"Everybody knows that you married a charity case like me to make yourself look like a good man," Melody said. "But that's not the real truth, is it?" Her voice was a whisper, at odds with the crash and burn inside her, her pounding heart, the giddy rush of her blood. "The real truth is that, deep down, you've always been a good man."

"You are sweet and naive," Griffin growled at her, and she could *feel* his words against her own lips. "Innocent and almost unimaginably vulnerable. Especially here, in this palace of games and pretenses."

Melody wanted to show him exactly how wrong he was about that, but somehow, she couldn't seem to move. As if he was in control of her body, not her.

Something that should have alarmed her. When instead it made her...light-headed.

"But beyond all of that," Griffin kept on, his voice laced with heat just like she was, and something like greed, "you're also wrong. You have no idea the things I want to do to you."

"Then do them," Melody managed to say. "I dare you."

Caitlin Crews

—

HIS SCANDALOUS
CHRISTMAS PRINCESS

HARLEQUIN

PRESENTS

HARLEQUIN®
PRESENTS®

Recycling programs
for this product may
not exist in your area.

ISBN-13: 978-1-335-89414-4

His Scandalous Christmas Princess

Copyright © 2020 by Caitlin Crews

This edition published by arrangement with Harlequin Books S.A.

For questions and comments about the quality of this book,
please contact us at CustomerService@Harlequin.com.

Harlequin Enterprises ULC
22 Adelaide St. West, 40th Floor
Toronto, Ontario M5H 4E3, Canada
www.Harlequin.com

Printed in U.S.A.

USA TODAY bestselling and RITA® Award–nominated author **Caitlin Crews** loves writing romance. She teaches her favorite romance novels in creative-writing classes at places like UCLA Extension's prestigious Writers' Program, where she finally gets to utilize the MA and PhD in English literature she received from the University of York in England. She currently lives in the Pacific Northwest with her very own hero and too many pets. Visit her at caitlincrews.com.

Books by Caitlin Crews

Harlequin Presents

The Italian's Pregnant Cinderella

Conveniently Wed!

My Bought Virgin Wife

One Night With Consequences

Secrets of His Forbidden Cinderella

Once Upon a Temptation

Claimed in the Italian's Castle

Secret Heirs of Billionaires

Unwrapping the Innocent's Secret

Royal Christmas Weddings

Christmas in the King's Bed

Visit the Author Profile page at Harlequin.com for more titles.

CHAPTER ONE

MELODY SKYROS HAD entertained herself for years by imagining that, at any moment, she could embrace her true destiny, become a deadly assassin, and go on a targeted killing spree of only those who really, really deserved it.

But that wouldn't be ladylike.

She had trained in various martial arts for years. In secret, thanks to one of her gently bred, blue-blooded mother's few acts of marital defiance. Because Melody's notoriously unpleasant father, aristocrat and media magnate Aristotle Skyros, could never know that his despised second daughter was receiving anything but the basic comportment classes expected of Idylla's lofty patricians, who cluttered up the ancient island kingdom with enough hereditary snobbishness to fill the gleaming Aegean Sea.

Aristotle could certainly never know that a

daughter of his had been training less in how to sit gracefully at a formal dinner and more in how to neutralize multiple attackers with her fingertips.

He had never forgiven her for being born flawed. He never would. Melody was blind and therefore useless to him—except as a weapon to wield against those who actually cared about her.

Melody's earliest, happiest daydreams of what she could do with the lethal skills she was learning and then mastering had all been focused on ridding the world of Aristotle.

Who most definitely deserved it.

But her older sister Calista had handled her father, shockingly enough. Calista, born perfect enough to please Aristotle, had worked her way up to become her father's second in the family corporation, all with an eye toward beating him at his own game. And sure enough, she'd embarrassed and humiliated him by having him removed from his own board and summarily fired from his position as CEO two days ago.

This was in no way as neat, clean, or personally satisfying a solution as an assassination, in Melody's opinion.

Especially when Melody was the one who

had to pay the price of Aristotle's embarrassment.

Though the price in question had its own rewards, she could admit.

Because tonight she had a new target in mind: His Royal Highness Prince Griffin of Idylla, who was her brand-new brother-in-law, since her sister had married King Orion the night before.

That was bad enough. Melody was still having trouble processing what else the famously oversexed and dissipated Griffin was. To her, personally.

Because it had all happened so fast. Too fast. *Dizzyingly* fast.

After Calista had become the Queen, the King had swept her off to the tune of cheers and much merriment as the clock in the palace struck midnight. Christmas Eve had ended, Christmas had begun. Glad tidings were exchanged on high, as befit the traditional, arranged marriage of an Idyllian king that Melody knew included deep and genuine emotion on both sides.

It only took a few moments in Orion and Calista's presence to *feel* how much they adored each other. A good and proper fairy tale that the whole kingdom could rejoice in and a balm for a nation wearied by the squalid, scandalous antics of Orion's predecessor, the deeply polluted King Max.

Orion had promised—since long before he took the throne—that his reign would be scandal-free.

When a palace aide had come to escort her away, Melody had assumed she'd be packed off home to her parents' house, where her father would no doubt be up waiting for her—keen to make her tell him every detail about the wedding and then punish her for attending it. She'd been looking forward to it, as matching wits with her father was one of her favorite games. He always assumed he was the smartest man in any room when, in fact, he was woefully unarmed.

Instead, she had been whisked off to a suite in the palace, something she found pleasant enough until she realized she'd been *locked in.* And come morning, her sister had emerged from what should have been newly wedded bliss to make her *announcements.*

"This is about making sure you're free, Melody," she'd said over breakfast. Sternly. Taking to her new role a bit too eagerly, in Melody's view. They'd sat in a private salon so sunny that Melody had leaned back in her chair, the bitter coffee she preferred between her hands, and tilted her face toward the heat of it.

"Are you sure? Because to me it sounds like a royal decree. *Your Majesty.*"

"It's both."

Calista sounded the way she always did, stressed and *sisterly* and racked with *grave concerns*. Melody never had the heart to tell her that she enjoyed her life a whole lot more than anyone—including Calista, who unlike the rest loved her dearly and was thus forgiven her unnecessary *concern*—seemed to imagine. That didn't suit most people's view of what blindness must be like, Melody was well aware. She had learned to keep it to herself.

"I appreciate your help, of course," Melody had told her. "But I don't need it. You shouldn't be worrying about such things, Calista. It's the first day of your new life as the Queen of Idylla, all hail. Not to mention, it's Christmas."

"I know it's Christmas," Calista had retorted, but her voice was softer. "And once a few practicalities are sorted out, I promise you that we'll celebrate the way we always do."

"You mean, with Father drunk and belligerent, shouting down the place around our ears while we all cower until January?" Melody had laughed. "As appealing as that sounds, maybe it's time for new traditions."

"But tonight is the Christmas ball," Calista had continued, sounding ever more dogged. Melody could feel the daggers her older sister was glaring at her, and, she could admit, took pleasure in remaining as placid and unbothered as possible. Because it annoyed Calista so deeply and obviously. "And I want to give you a gift that no one, least of all Father, can ever take back."

That Melody had not wanted this gift was neither here nor there.

"I think I'd rather take my chances with Father's temper," Melody had said when Calista had told her what she wanted Melody to do.

What she, as Queen, had *decreed* Melody *would* do, that was.

"You can't," her sister had replied. "If you go home again he will ship you off to one of those institutions he's been threatening you with for years. It might as well be a prison, Melody! And it's unlikely that he will ever let you out again. Do you hear me?"

"My ears work perfectly well, Calista. As I think you know."

But the new Queen had made up her mind. That was how Melody had found herself in the arms of Prince Griffin, Idylla's so-called *charming rogue* as he led her in an excruciatingly formal and horrifically *long* dance in the Grand Ballroom of the palace.

Prince Griffin, who was forgiven his many sins and trespasses in the style of his father because he was considered *delightful*, for reasons unclear to Melody.

Prince Griffin, who had declared he planned to turn over a new leaf to better support his brother back during coronation season, but had taken his sweet time in the turning.

Prince Griffin, her new assassination target.

And to her dismay, as of an hour or so ago, her husband.

Melody had considered knifing him in the back at the altar, for the poetry of it all, but Prince Griffin—renowned across the land for his cavorting about with any and all women, his cheerful debauchery, and his disinterest in the usual charitable pursuits of royalty that were usually erected to cover up the consequences of the first two—was under the impression that he was Melody's…protector.

She would have been only too happy to disabuse him of this notion. But that, too, had been forbidden.

By yet another royal decree.

"Don't be absurd," Melody had said, while she'd stood gamely still in another of the palace's innumerable salons. She'd been subjecting herself to a phalanx of dressmakers, all of whom poked and prodded and pinned her into a dress she had not wanted to wear at all, and certainly not after the extraordinarily formal Christmas lunch she'd eaten her way through. "I have no need or desire for protection. Prince Griffin's or anyone else's."

Her sister and her new husband had been there, lounging about in their post-Christmas luncheon haze. And perhaps post–private time haze as well, though Melody knew her supposedly hard-as-nails, professional sister was enormously missish about such things. At least to Melody.

As if her eyes were the not the only thing that did not function as expected.

Everything smelled sugary and sweet, floating up toward the high ceilings. And over the mutterings of the vicious dressmakers and their sharp, cruel pins she could hear various rustles from the settee the King and his new Queen sat upon. Telling her there was a lot of *touching*. Perhaps more touching than had been seen in the palace for some time.

"I know you don't need any protection,"

Calista had replied, but in a tone of voice that suggested to Melody that her sister was rolling her eyes. "But it's not about you, you see."

"The forced wedding I want no part of is not about me?" Melody asked. Rhetorically, obviously. "And here I thought it was meant to answer my dreams of becoming a princess at last. Not a dream I've ever had, to be clear."

She heard her sister sigh. She heard the King shift position.

Orion was a different order of man than Melody's father. Or his own father, come to that, or the country could never have embraced him. Not after the things Terrible King Max had done and laughed about when they'd turned up in the tabloids, as they inevitably did. That Orion was fully in control of himself—and therefore everything else—was palpable. Comforting in a king.

As someone who'd spent her entire life learning how to control herself in various ways, physical and mental and more, Melody was forced to admire him.

"Your sister has regaled me with tales of your abilities," Orion had said then. Melody had felt the astonishing urge to offer him the appropriate obeisance. Not that she could with so many people around her, pinning and prodding and demanding she remain still. She was surprised she even had the urge to drop a curtsy, but there it was. The first time in her whole life she'd actually felt decidedly patriotic. "And I'm delighted that my brother will take such a remarkable woman as his bride. But you must understand something about Griffin."

Melody had felt certain that she understood Prince Griffin all too well. The spare had not followed in the footsteps of the heir. Griffin had always preferred gambling halls, the beds of unsuitable women, and any other form of debauchery available to him. And as a royal prince, there was very little that was *not* available to him. He was not the sort of man who would require *work* to figure out. Melody had been bored of him and his high-profile antics long before she'd ever met him.

This was something she would have said happily to her sister. But Orion was not only the King, he was Griffin's brother. So, uncharacteristically, she'd remained politely silent.

"He has always played a certain role, particularly with women," said the King, and somehow, Melody had kept herself from letting out an inelegant snort. *A certain role* was one way to describe an unrepentant libertine who had spent the better part of his life knee-deep in conquests. "But with you, he is…different."

This was true, but not for the reasons Orion likely imagined. It had always amused Melody to cringe about and act as if she might crumble to dust if someone paid attention to her. It gave her great satisfaction to allow people she could easily have maimed to fawn all over her and treat her as if she was too damaged to sit without assistance.

In other words, she'd long enjoyed acting the part of damaged goods.

The first time she'd met Prince Griffin, it had been second nature to act as if his mere presence was enough to give her the vapors. As if her blindness made her timid and she could do nothing but quail and cower.

Melody did so enjoy being underestimated.

Until now.

"I would take it as a personal favor if you would allow my brother to imagine that he can, in fact, protect you. Not because you need protection, but because I believe it would do him good to indulge that feeling." Orion sighed. "I ask you this, not as your King, but as his brother."

What could Melody do with that but acquiesce?

She had not knifed Prince Griffin at the

altar, though it had caused her pain to refrain. She had even smiled—if tremulously, the way the person the Prince thought she was would smile, surely—though that was something she usually avoided doing in public. Her father always raged at her that she should smile more, so, naturally, she had taken it upon herself to smile as seldomly as possible. When Prince Griffin had finally led her into the ballroom, it was as his supposedly submissive and overwhelmed wife. His charity case.

It had been the longest, strangest Christmas of Melody's life.

So long and so strange that she found herself almost nostalgic for the usual Skyros family Christmases past. Idyllians tended to reserve the gift-giving for Boxing Day and then again in January on Epiphany, the feast of the three wise men. Christmas was for the traditional breads, walnuts, and pork or lamb, depending on the family. In her own family, Christmas was one of the few occasions Melody's mother insisted her father acknowledge that Melody existed, which made for a long, fraught, unpleasant meal that likely gave everyone indigestion, reliably left at least one member of the family in tears, and inevitably ended with smashed china and threats.

That sounded like a lovely Christmas carol

in comparison to this, she thought as she was introduced to the King, the palace, and then the watching nation as the kingdom's newest Princess.

Then came the interminable dancing.

"You are remarkably good at this," the Prince told her, as he waltzed them both around and around and around.

Melody was entirely too aware of the pressure of so many pairs of eyes on them. The *weight* of it all. And the murmuring and whispering and muffled laughter, snaking about beneath the music, as all the gathered Idyllian nobles attempted to come to terms with what shouldn't have been possible.

Everybody's favorite prince, married to the damaged, discarded, scandalous-by-virtue-of-her-notable-imperfections daughter of the already highly questionable Skyros family. Yes, Calista had done well for herself. But Aristotle was a stain on the kingdom. Everyone agreed—until they wanted to do business with him.

Well. Not any longer, perhaps. There was that silver lining to hold on to.

Melody found dancing silly. It was so much more pleasurable—and effective—to fight. But the simpering creature, fragile and overwhelmed, that she was playing tonight would never think such a thing.

Nor have the tools to fight in the first place, she reminded herself.

She shivered dramatically, hoping Prince Griffin would imagine it was fear.

"I hope I don't embarrass you," she said, in a quavering sort of voice. The kind of voice she liked to use around her father, mostly because it always made her sister laugh. And usually also made her father choke with rage that such a daughter had been inflicted upon him. "I couldn't bear it if I embarrassed you."

Prince Griffin was tall. His shoulder was broad and remarkably firm to the touch. Much as his mouth had been when he'd kissed her, swift and perfunctory, as the wedding ceremony had ended. The hand that grasped hers was large, and dwarfed her fingers in a manner both powerful and gentle. Its mate was splayed across her back, pressing heat into her with every step of the dance.

Years ago, when she and her sister were still teenagers, Calista had spent untold hours describing various members of the royal and aristocratic circles their family moved in. Painting each and every character for Melody, who had her own impressions of them based on how they took up space, how they breathed, how they fidgeted and smelled. But even if Calista had not exhaustively detailed Prince Griffin's wicked gaze and shockingly sensual mouth long ago, these things were apparent in the way he carried himself. The way he spoke, his voice rich and deep. And more curious, capable of stirring up something…electrical.

Deep within her.

Melody didn't know what to make of that.

"You could never embarrass me," Prince Griffin said gallantly. "I have spent far too many years embarrassing myself."

And while part of Melody wanted to laugh at that, there was another part of her that… shuddered. Deep inside, where that electricity seemed to hum louder than before.

It was almost alarming.

The orchestra was still playing. And as was tradition and ancient royal protocol, the newlyweds were required to dance to the bitter end. On display, so all of Idylla could form its own conclusions about the new couple before the tabloids took them apart come morning.

Given that Melody was the daughter of a media king who had long trafficked in tabloids as a matter of course and a means to shame his enemies and rivals, she expected there would be quite the tabloid commotion tomorrow. On Boxing Day, when the whole of the island would be tucked up at home opening gifts, stuffing themselves with food, and perfectly situated to read, watch, and judge.

Judgment being the foremost occupation of most of the island's citizens, as far as Melody had ever been able to tell.

The dance finally ended. Mercifully.

But Prince Griffin did not release Melody's hand.

Instead, he placed it in the crook of his elbow, a courtly sort of gesture that Melody, by rights, should have found annoying. She did find it annoying, she assured herself. She did not need to be ushered about like an invalid. She only used a cane sparingly—and usually for effect—having spent so many years working to hone her other senses and her spatial awareness through martial arts. Because she loved the notion that she could be as graceful as any other Idyllian lady, when and if she wished.

She reminded herself that tonight's show of weakness wasn't about her. It was about the man beside her, who needed the King to intercede on his behalf. Who needed his brother to not only arrange his marriage, but make his new wife complicit in pulling one over on him. For his own good.

Something in Melody twisted a bit at that. She knew the particular, crushing weight of *her own good* better than most. It had threatened to flatten her for most of her life.

But she reminded herself that Prince Griffin was a stranger. That she had done what was asked of her, that was all. He was the King's brother—but *she* was nothing but the King's lowly subject.

That didn't make the twist in her belly go away. But it helped.

The night wore on. Griffin stayed at her side, which meant Melody had no choice but to smile. To simper. To pretend to be *overwrought* by her remarkable elevation in status.

When instead, what she really was, she found, was…entertained.

Not just by this stranger, this husband foisted upon her, who acted as if she needed him to dote on her in this way. But by all the women who contrived reasons to swan up and *congratulate* Prince Griffin on his nuptials.

And it was him they were congratulating, Melody was well aware. Not her. They all seemed to suffer from the same common ailment—the notion that because Melody couldn't see them, she also couldn't hear them.

They came to him in clouds of scent, their voices dripping with greed. Malicious intent. And when aimed at Melody, nothing short of pure disdain.

"I'm so deeply happy for you, Your Royal Highness," they would flutter at him. "But how hard it is to imagine one such as you truly off the market."

"Do you mean the local farmers' markets?" Melody would ask, disingenuously. And tried to beam just slightly angled away from the direction of whatever woman stood before her. "I am told they've made such a difference in the city center. So festive, particularly at this time of year."

Perhaps her favorite part of the whole thing was standing there in the aftermath of such fatuous statements, feeling the reaction all around her.

Oh, yes, she was enjoying herself.

She would never have chosen to marry of her own volition. But having been forced into it, and having received an order from King Orion to play a part, Melody found the whole thing far more amusing than she'd expected.

Until the trumpets blared and it was her turn to be swept out of the ballroom by her royal husband.

Melody wanted to complain at length to

her sister, because no one else knew her well enough to listen to her without simultaneously pitying her in some way she would likely find deeply tiresome. But the Queen was not available for sisterly grousing, leaving Melody to surrender herself to this last part of the royal marriage ritual while keeping her feelings to herself.

She thought this particular part of the traditional Idyllian royal wedding was cringeworthy. Everyone stood about as if they were in some medieval keep, cheering on the bridegroom as he ushered his new wife off to what they claimed was *happy-after-ever*.

What they meant was *the marital bed*.

Melody had never understood these strange architectures erected around sex. In the case of a royal wedding, everyone pretended it was about courtly manners. Or ceremony. Or tradition itself, as if the fact people had long done something meant everyone must forever carry on doing it.

But at the end of all the theatrics, it was about sex. It was always about sex. It amused her to no end that *she* seemed to be the only person capable of seeing that.

Prince Griffin drew her along with him and because Melody could not comment on this the way she would have liked, she had no choice but to…allow it.

And there was suddenly nothing to concentrate on but him. Awareness swept over her, whether she wanted it or not.

He was hot to the touch. Too hot. He had a hand splayed at her low back again and she wished he would remove it, because it was far too…confusing.

Distracting.

She told herself it was because they were climbing stairs. That was why she seemed to be heating up, almost steaming. But deep inside, low in her belly, it was if her body was far more exultantly medieval than she'd ever imagined possible.

He moved with a certain quiet power that made the fine hairs on the back of her neck prickle. Because she recognized it. He was… contained. Not quite what he seemed on the surface. And she could feel that so distinctly it was as if he was making announcements to that effect as he led her away from the crowd.

He kept a firm, if gentle, hold of her, as if she needed help navigating through the wide corridors of the palace and their acres and acres of gleaming, empty marble. He did not make small talk, and when she noticed that, it made all the strange things churning about inside her start to glow.

Because the character of Prince Griffin that everybody knew so well had never let a moment go by without filling it with sound of his own voice. Everyone knew that. Notorious charmers were rarely shy and retiring.

Not that she thought the real Prince Griffin, whoever he might be, was *shy*. The quality of his silence was different than that. It was too confident. Too secure.

She could feel it in the way he guided her, with an ease that suggested he'd spent the bulk of his life matching his pace to hers and maneuvering her where he wanted her, and this wasn't the first night he'd ever done so. It felt so natural it was almost as if she was leading the way.

Melody understood, deep in her bones, that this was not a man to be trifled with.

But she couldn't make that odd glimmer of understanding work with the fact he was *Prince Griffin*, so she shoved it aside. And pretended she was flushed from the walking in such a cumbersome gown, nothing more.

Instead of taking her toward the guest suite where she'd been put up the night before, he headed in a completely different direction. And paying attention to him was too disconcerting, so instead, she paid attention to the direction they moved in. A long walk, then left. Down a set of stairs, then out into a courtyard. There was a fountain making noise, and she could hear the sound of the water bounce back from the walls.

Then she remembered. Prince Griffin did not live in a wing of the palace, the way his brother did. He maintained his own residence on the far side of the palace grounds.

She could feel the press of the December night, chilly for Idylla, though mitigated by blasts of heat at equal intervals as they walked. Heaters, no doubt. Because royal personages could not be expected to suffer the travails of weather.

Melody wanted to laugh at that. But didn't, because it occurred to her that she was now one of those royal personages. Like it or not.

Then they were inside again. His home, she understood. Hers, now. There was the scent of him, or something that reminded her of him. A certain richness, a hint of intensity. She could sense walls around her, suggesting an entry hall, and then a room. He led her to a couch, placing her hand on the arm and encouraging her to sit. She ran her fingers over the wide arm of the couch, done up in a deep, sumptuous leather. Then she sank down on the seat, tossing the skirt of her enormous dress out as she settled into place, and getting a sense of the width of the couch as she did.

And then she listened.

Her husband moved almost silently. So silently, in fact, that it once again made her shiver in the grip of too much awareness. She had the sense of him prowling, and he was...

Not the same, here.

Away from the crowds, something in her whispered.

Was this where Prince Griffin was truly himself? Whatever that meant?

That electric charge deep inside her connected again, lighting her up. Sending heat and flame and something else shivering through all parts of her body, making her want to leap to her feet to do something to dispel it—

But instead, she reminded herself to be meek. This was not where *she* could be herself. She could only play her prescribed part, as ordered. Melody bowed her head.

And listened as her surprisingly formidable Prince—her husband, God help her—fixed himself a drink. Then one for her too, she corrected herself, as she heard ice hit heavy crystal for a second time.

Sure enough, he was soon beside her again, pressing a cool tumbler into her palm.

"I thought we could both use a bit of whiskey," he said, in a low sort of growl that bore almost no resemblance at all to the cultured, charming, carefree tone he'd used in the ballroom as all those women had vied for his attention.

It was fascinating. *He* was.

Melody felt herself flush.

"I want you to be comfortable here," Prince Griffin told her, still sounding growly, but with a more formal note mixed in. "And you have nothing to fear from me. I do not intend to…insist upon any marital rights."

Her flush deepened. She told herself it was outrage that he would even mention *marital rights* in the twenty-first century. But she knew better.

If she was outraged at anything, it was that he'd apparently decided his own wife didn't merit the same sexual attention he was literally famous for flinging about like it was confetti. Without even asking if, perhaps, she might like to partake of the one thing he was widely held to be any good at.

"Why not?" Melody demanded. Then remembered herself. She tried to exude innocence and fragility, and only hoped she didn't look constipated in the process. "Forgive me if I'm misunderstanding the situation we find ourselves in here. But I thought the entire purpose of these royal weddings with all the protocol and the carrying on about bloodlines and history was the sex?"

took consummated in the process. Forgive me
if I'm neglecting the manual on we luxe
ourselves to have. But I thought the entire
purpose of these royal weddings, with all the
pomp and the carryon on about bloodlines
and heritage...

CHAPTER TWO

His Royal Highness, Prince Griffin of Idylla,
could not possibly have heard his frail and
fragile new bride correctly.

He stared down at her, trying to make
sense of the question that was, as far as he
could tell, still hanging in the air between
them. Filling up his private study, stealing all
the air out of the room, and most disconcert-
ingly by far, centering itself between his legs.

Where, it appeared, his body had already
decided that he was attracted to his wife.

Wildly attracted.

Griffin was appalled.

At himself for proving, as ever, he was
more monster than man.

Lady Melody Skyros was not only a gently
reared noblewoman, deserving of his respect
and care. She was not merely one of Idylla's
sweet young things whose mothers plotted
exquisite marriages like something out of a

period film while their fathers vied for power and influence. She was also blind. His choosing to marry her was, as he was well aware, an act of largesse that palace insiders believed would redeem him in one fell swoop in the eyes of the populace.

She was his redemption, in other words.

Griffin did not want to think about sex. Not with her. Not near her.

His tawdry exploits were in the past. Melody was his future.

The past was dirty, just as he'd liked it, but the future—as he'd promised his brother—would be squeaky clean.

Griffin was many things and pretended to be many more, but his word was his bond. Always.

And when he slipped and thought about sex in the presence of this woman he barely knew who was now his for all time, it became entirely too difficult to keep ignoring the fact that she was beautiful.

Inarguably, impossibly, shockingly beautiful.

The kind of beautiful that could, if he let it, lead straight to very bad decisions on Griffin's part. The sort of decisions he absolutely could not permit himself to make any longer. He'd promised Orion those days were behind him.

Because they were, he assured himself. Sternly. This was Orion's squeaky-clean new future and Griffin had vowed he would do his part.

Even if his part meant living like a monk in the presence of an angel.

"I cannot have heard you correctly," he managed to say, clenching his tumbler of whiskey tight in his hand.

Too tight.

"Sex leading to the required royal heirs, of course," Melody said in that same sweet voice that matched her name and seemed to get tangled up inside him. "I am given to understand that every person on the island of Idylla with even the faintest trace of noble blood thinks of nothing *but* heirs."

Griffin coughed. He forced himself to look away. He even went and sat down in the chair across from her to put some more distance between them, but that was not an improvement.

The view was still the same.

Lady Melody was widely held to be the embarrassment of her family. The Skyros Scandal—though it was not so much that she was personally scandalous as that her obvious imperfections had so clearly and deeply offended her father. Because heaven forfend any creature on this island be anything less than physically perfect. Especially if that creature happened to be related to a bottom-feeder like Aristotle Skyros who trafficked in the mythic beauty of the Idyllian population.

A myth his own media outlets perpetuated, naturally.

And all the while he'd had his own blind daughter locked away, out of view unless absolutely unavoidable.

Rumors had always swirled about the younger, lesser Skyros daughter. Was she misshapen? Incapable of human interaction? One salacious story had claimed, for years, that the ironically named youngest child of well-known snob Aristotle was, in fact, a monster he kept chained up in his basement. Her sister had been in the public eye from a young age, following in her father's footsteps and rising in the Skyros family empire. And then, of course, her father and the former King had arranged to marry Calista to Orion in a seedy little conspiracy of force.

It was as if Calista had to shine all the brighter—all the way to the throne—to divert attention from the whispers of deformities and insanities and monstrous rampages in the dark of night.

Even when Melody had appeared at the series of balls leading up to her sister's wedding on Christmas Eve—notably neither deformed nor monstrous—the gossip had continued.

All absurd, of course, but Idylla was a relatively small island. Where larger kingdoms had cities, the people here had their stories.

Griffin had expected that perhaps Melody would not have the polish of her older sister. Who could? Calista was in so many ways a sharpened blade. Anyone would seem rough around the edges in comparison.

But today there was no escaping the truth. Melody was a vision.

He had seen her from across a ballroom, once or twice, as a distant curiosity. And up close only once before. That time her blond hair had cascaded all around her while huddled in a chair, trying to make herself invisible while her sister prepared to become Queen. His memory of her at that brief meeting—a bit like an urchin, Eponine to the gills—had stayed with him over this last, strange week, when it became clear that he could no longer put off doing his duty.

And it had been that memory that made him feel…not resigned, exactly, to this plan of his brother's that he'd vowed to support. Griffin had no wish to marry. But if it turned out that he must do so anyway, he found he could see his way clear to marrying a woebegone creature like the one he'd seen that day. A victim to her overbearing father, the subject of idle gossip and absurd stories. Blind, ignored, possibly even abused.

He would *elevate* her, he had told himself grandly even last night. He would *take care* of her. There would be no lies like the ones that had shaped his life—not in his marriage. And perhaps, somewhere deep inside himself, he would find something soft after all these years of bitterness and hardness. Something that might bloom instead of wither.

Something good, even in him.

A thing he'd lost so long ago that he'd begun to think it, too, was nothing more than a myth. But then his bride had appeared down at the other end of the long aisle of the Grand Cathedral. And she had walked the length of it on his brother's arm, far too graceful for a charity case. Far too…frothy.

Beneath her veil, he'd expected to find the sad, cringing waif he'd met so briefly once before.

But instead, there had been…this.

Her.

Melody, something in him whispered.

All that blond hair gleamed gold, piled

on top of her head and fixed into place with gleaming precious stones set on elegant combs that gave the impression of a tiara without actually using one. A tiara could make an ordinary face exciting, simply by adding all that light and sparkle, but Melody's face was already exquisite. Heart-shaped, with eyes that he had half expected—based on what, he didn't know—to be clouded over. Strange in some way. But instead, they gleamed like his beloved sea. And her neck was a graceful, aristocratic line, signposting the rest of her slender, supple form beneath the dress she wore that was more like spun sugar than fabric.

She looked like a fairy tale.

And Griffin did not believe in fairy tales.

Eyes like the ocean, lips like rubies—and what the hell was he doing?

"I have no particular need of heirs," he managed to say, recollecting himself. And more important, the vows he'd made to protect this woman from harm—and himself. "And therefore no need to marry to procure them."

Much less to procure access to the mechanism by which heirs were produced.

Did Melody not know who he was?

If there had been witnesses to this conversation, which there mercifully were not, they would not have believed it. *The* Prince Griffin, reduced to this state? After his years in the military alone, when he had faced far greater challenges than a beautiful woman who wished to talk about sex he would not be having with her.

To say nothing of his dedication to sampling as many women as possible, and not to *talk*.

About *heirs*.

Until tonight, he would have said that there was no way a woman could surprise him. No chance.

And yet here he was.

"That can't be true, Your Royal Highness."

His bride managed to sound as if the gently chiding statement was actually a question. Her face was tilted toward the tumbler she held in her delicate hands, where a ring that had once been his mother's dwarfed her slender finger. It was not the ring his despised father had given his poor mother on the occasion of their traditionally arranged royal wedding. This ring, she had told him long before her sad end, had been handed down through her own aristocratic family. It had once belonged to his great-great-grandmother, herself a great favorite of a long-gone Idyllian prince.

It felt like a talisman. When Orion had announced Griffin's time was up, he'd gone and found the ring, pleased with its weight, its heft. It was a recognizable gift of his esteem that he could bestow upon this charity case of his, bedecking her and marking her as his own.

Last night, his final evening as a free man, he had rather liked imagining it on her finger. It had felt like an internal settling within him. A quiet reckoning. He had felt ready—almost eager—to begin this next chapter.

In which he would play a new role. That of a good man like his brother, rather than the kingdom's favorite scoundrel.

Griffin had been *alight* with his own nascent virtue.

Yet something about this woman and that ring *here*, in his private study where she spoke of sex and not gratitude, moved through him...differently.

And felt too much like heat.

Griffin shoved that aside as best he could. "I am many things, Lady Melody. There is no pretending otherwise. But I am not a liar."

A curious sort of smile curved her lips, though she kept her face tilted toward the glass she held. Angled so he could not quite read her expression.

"And I am not a lady." Her smile looked innocent again. Very nearly tremulous. He found himself frowning, as if something about her wasn't quite tracking. "As of tonight I am Her Royal Highness, Princess Melody of Idylla. Your brother said so himself."

"Indeed you are."

"I will confess to you that I did not harbor secret dreams of becoming a princess. I am told most girls do, but then, I was never much like *most girls*."

Griffin thought of monsters and dark basements, images that did not fit with the elegant creature before him, all gold and ivory and that mysterious curve to her mouth besides. "I should hope not. I doubt I could bring myself to marry *most girls*."

He expected her to flush with pleasure. For her smile to tip over into something... more recognizable, maybe. Certainly more pleased with her circumstances. Or him. Or even herself.

But it stayed as it was. Innocent and yet... not.

And that ring on her hand like a harbinger.

Griffin was no doubt overwrought. He tossed back the healthy measure of the whiskey in his glass and ordered himself to stop looking for myth when there was nothing but a marriage. What did he expect? He had never been married before. It was not an institution he had ever intended to experience personally. Not after witnessing his parents' ritual abuse of the sanctity of their own union.

Or, as he liked to call it, his fondest childhood memories. All of them lies of one sort or another.

And if *he* was finding forbearance hard to come by tonight, what must it be like for Melody? She might not have been chained in a basement, but she had been sheltered all the same. In the most literal sense.

He needed to think less about his own contradictory feelings and more about what she must be feeling, ripped out of the only home she knew. Even if that home had been with the vile Aristotle Skyros, change was always hard.

Griffin ordered himself to be benevolent. Wasn't that the point of all this?

"I know that wedding nights are more typically spent in baser pursuits," he said, aware as he spoke that it was still as if he was…outside his skin somehow. He rubbed at his face, suddenly more relieved than he should have been that this new bride of his who was unsettling him so comprehensively couldn't actually *see* her handiwork. He knew he should have hated himself for that, but there was far too long a list already. "But that is not something that need concern us. I will not impose upon you, if you were worried. You can rest easy on that score."

There was a pause.

Griffin heard a loud noise and it took him far too long to realize it was his own pulse, a racket in his ears.

As if he was the person panicked tonight. He, who was renowned for his calm under any and all pressures.

His bride curved her lips into something small and demure. "You are too good."

He found himself studying her again, because he didn't believe that smile. Not when she'd sounded so…dry. Or was he imbuing her with a personality that would better suit that heat in him that he was doing his best to keep tamped down?

You're terrible at charity, Griffin growled at himself, which was not exactly news. *The poor thing is no doubt petrified. Focus on that, not yourself, if you can.*

"I'm aware I have a certain reputation," he said, as gently as he could. Because perhaps it was best to address everything head-on. To have the sort of conversation most people— even people in arranged marriages like his—

surely had before taking their vows, even if the topic was business or wealth and property consolidation in lieu of poetry or romance. Not that it mattered much when the end result would be the same. "I want to make sure you know that you will never have to bear the burden of it."

"Is it burdensome?" Again, that dry tone when her face better resembled that of a distant saint carved into marble. Or, more likely, he was hallucinating that contradiction in her because he was self-serving to the core. If Griffin had any virtue at all, it was that he knew himself too well. "I was always under the impression that you enjoyed yourself. Thoroughly."

"The burden was not mine, Melody." Her name in his mouth…did not help. "It was my brother's. He wished to promise the kingdom that the royal family was reformed. But it was not Orion who needed reforming."

"You are very kind to reorder your life to please your brother. Even if he is the King."

"I was under the impression you did much the same for your sister."

"Didn't you hear?" Melody's voice was light. Yet ironic, he would have said—had she been anyone else. "She was doing me the favor."

"The honor is mine," he said, inclining his head slightly as if she could see his courtly gestures.

He knew she couldn't. Yet the way she tilted her head slightly to one side almost made him wonder.

"You are too kind, Your Royal Highness."

"We are wed." His voice was starched straight through. "You must call me Griffin."

"Griffin, then."

And they both sat there a moment. She looked as remote as she did beautiful. He found himself wondering what on earth he'd gotten himself into.

He did not think about the way she'd said his name.

Melody turned her glass in her hand, but not as if she was fidgeting. It was more as if she was...considering it. That didn't make sense. "If our marriage is in name only, does that mean that you will continue your... ah... exploits as before?"

For a moment, Griffin forgot who she was. For a moment, this was no more and no less than a dance he knew far better than the waltz they'd performed in front of the world.

All his good intentions seemed to ignite.

"Are you asking me if I intend to keep my wedding vows?" he asked with a certain silken menace. "Or are you more interested in discussing my exploits?"

As if she was the latest woman auditioning to warm his bed, and nothing more.

He could feel his pulse again, greedy and intent. And across from him, he was sure he saw a flicker of something sensual move across her face, lighting her up and making every last muscle in his body tighten—

But he was mistaken. He had to be.

Because, while he watched, she seemed to shrink there across from him. No saintliness, no sensuality, only a crumpling in on herself.

It was unbearable.

He was truly everything they said he was, and more. Bitter as that was, Griffin had no choice but to accept it.

Look at what you're doing here, he growled at himself. *You can't help yourself.*

"Am I allowed to question you?" Her voice was the same thread of sound he remembered from before, when he'd seen his future Queen's blind waif of a sister and had found himself seized with the uncharacteristic urge to protect her. "I'm so sorry. I'm afraid I hardly know how to handle myself in the presence of a man of your stature. Or at all. I must confess to you that I have not often been in…anyone's company, really."

She sounded plaintive. Uncertain and overwhelmed. By contrast, Griffin felt himself relax. He felt on solid ground again.

This, he could do. He was not a monster like his father. King Max had been a dark man, bent and determined to demean and degrade, use and discard. He had been venal and greedy.

Griffin was none of those things. He indulged in his sins, yes. But he didn't wield them as weapons.

Looking at this lovely, infinitely breakable creature who had become his wife, he reminded himself that this was his chance. At last he, too, could be virtuous.

Without actually having to dedicate himself to all those tiresome years of self-control and abstinent moral rectitude that defined his brother.

All he needed to do was be kind.

Surely even he could manage that.

"You can do or say whatever you like," he assured her, almost indulgently. "This is your home now. And to make it more appealing for you, your sister made certain that I engaged your favorite aide to ease the transition. I hope that, in time, you will be happy here." He reminded himself that he was not taking in a delicate boarder. He was talking about a marriage. "With me."

Melody cleared her throat delicately. "My aide?"

"I'm told she was responsible for privately tutoring you in all the tedious rules of Idyllian comportment. And then stayed on afterward as you enjoyed her companionship."

His bride's face glowed. Again, Griffin felt filled with a new sort of joy.

He could do this. He could be the man he'd never been.

"I enjoy her companionship very much," Melody said, emotion clear in her voice.

When she sat up straight again, Griffin felt as if he'd won something.

"Inside the walls of this house, you can do as you please," he told her. "Think of it as yours. You will have your own apartments. All the independence you might crave. All I ask is that outside these walls, you never let anyone know the truth about our relationship."

The glow on her face faded a bit, and he disliked it. Intensely.

"But everyone will know the truth as soon as you return to your usual…pursuits." She did not *quite* shrug. "People like to gossip in general, I think, but gossiping about you is a national pastime."

It was said so innocently. He couldn't possibly object.

And still, his grip on his tumbler was so tight that he was briefly concerned that he would shatter the glass.

Because no one seemed to think he would keep his word. Not Orion. Not his lovely new wife.

Not you? asked a voice inside him. Mocking him.

Reminding him who he really was.

"I will not be returning to any 'pursuits,'" he gritted out.

Quite apart from having made vows to Melody, he had made a promise to his brother. His King.

Griffin released his grip on the glass, his gaze on his bride. "Idylla has seen more than its share of scandals. There will be no more. Not if I have anything to say about it."

And his new bride bent her head as if to curtsy before him, small and meek, and why was he having trouble with that? Why was he looking for more?

"Then it is as good as done," she said softly.

As if she was in danger of being carried off by the next breeze. "I am sure of it."

Griffin told himself he was, too.

"I hope everything in your rooms can your
...

CHAPTER THREE

MELODY AND HER brand-new, confusing
stranger of a husband were summoned—in-
vited, she kept reminding herself, though did
it count as an invitation when it couldn't be
refused?—to a "cozy" Boxing Day morning
with Their Royal Majesties, King Orion and
Queen Calista of Idylla.

In the palace proper, which was unlikely to
be *cozy* in any way. By definition.

Then again, it wasn't as if the holiday had
ever been filled with anything resembling
cheer in her parents' house, either. Or cozi-
ness. Or much in the way of goodwill toward
men—or anyone.

"I trust you find everything in your rooms
acceptable," Griffin said when he came to
collect her outside said rooms. "You must let
the staff know if anything does not suit you."

Even his voice sounded stiff and gruffly
awkward. Melody wasn't the least surprised

to find that when he once again guided her hand to grip his elbow, his entire body could have been confused for a column of granite.

As if he was the one who was out of place here, in this own home, instead of her.

Oddly, this made her feel more comfortable.

"I'm overcome by your generosity, Your Royal Highness," she said in as decent an impression of his wooden formality as she could muster up.

And then tried to remind herself that she was supposed to be awash in all her fraudulent cringing as he led her back toward the palace.

Half of her attention was on the route Griffin took, different from the night before. He went out the side of his house—*their* house, she corrected herself—and led her back into the courtyard that separated his residence from the palace. Melody breathed in deep, enjoying the faint, salt sting of the ocean breeze tinged with hints of far-off storms. And reveled in the chill in the air, in case she'd forgotten that it was December. She noticed the blasts of heat again, placed at clever intervals, just when she thought the winter chill might penetrate her skin.

She was keenly aware that Griffin was

walking at a deeply sedate pace that was almost certainly for her benefit, as he was far too tall. With, presumably, the long legs to match. He couldn't possibly consider this *procession* a reasonable pace. Melody tried to tell herself that it was kind of him to slow down in a misguided attempt to cater to her needs, whether she actually needed him to do it or not. It was something she ought to appreciate, surely.

It wasn't as if she'd had a lot of kindness, particularly from men. She ought to have been basking in any faint sign of it.

But she couldn't quite get there. Because the rest of her attention was focused on the deeply pleasurable, if unconventional, wedding night she'd had.

Griffin had delivered her to her rooms and then left her to her own devices. That had included a tray of food from his kitchens that she tore into the moment she finally freed herself from that enormous gown. Only when she'd finally eaten enough to stave off the hollow feeling in her belly after a long day of performing her fragility did she and Fen, her sensei and friend since Melody was small, set about learning each and every contour of her new home.

Fen had been old and wizened when she'd

started teaching Melody at the tender age of seven, or so she liked to claim. And as each year passed, she became more and more herself. *Earning the right to her bones*, she liked to say.

And what her bones liked the most that night was making sure Melody could navigate the house she found herself in with as much silent ease as she had her parents' home.

They'd started in Melody's rooms and then, when the household had gone quiet for the night, had fanned out to the rest of Prince Griffin's domain, taking it room by room, chamber by chamber, until Melody had memorized the layout of her new home as best she could on an initial sweep.

Then she and Fen had returned to their upgraded royal apartments and settled into their new and improved life of luxury.

"I am all right with this Prince," Fen said happily as she'd gone off to her own private room in Melody's suite. "So far."

"As am I," Melody had murmured as Fen's footsteps faded away, leaving her to her lovely new bedchamber, stocked with quietly elegant furnishings that warmed beneath her hands and complete with an honest-to-God fourposter bed with a princess canopy.

Nothing Melody had ever wanted or

dreamed of, necessarily. But she was happy to have it all the same, and with so little required of her in return.

This morning, both she and Fen had revised their charitable opinions somewhat when they'd discovered that in her new role as a royal princess, Melody was no longer expected or encouraged to dress herself.

Her staff—because, apparently, she had a *staff* in the royal version of her life—had first appeared to hover about and smother her with unsolicited and unnecessary help while she'd tried to get out of her wedding dress. They'd appeared again that morning, three relentlessly cheerful women who would not take no for an answer. Instead, they'd bustled ferociously around the vast apartment, which would have resulted in their quick and merciless deaths at Melody's hand had they not come bearing a tray of Idyllian pastries to complement the thick, rich coffee that had far more in common with traditional Greek coffee than the milky, frothy concoctions preferred in other places. Or so Melody had read.

Even Fen's dark mutterings of the dire consequences she might mete out for waking her were soothed away with an infusion of caffeine. And lashings of butter and dough.

Melody had found that shoving bits of

heavenly pastry in her mouth was the only way that she could make it through the experience of having more women flutter about her. Dressing her as if she was an oversize doll. It was creepy.

"I am only going to my sister's house," she said at one point, when she could no longer keep her words trapped inside her. And what came out was far more polite than what still lurked around in there. "We've spent many, many hours together wearing only our pajamas. I'm not sure this level of preparation is called for."

"I can't imagine that anyone would wish to go before Their Royal Majesties without looking their absolute best," one of the women said. Mildly enough.

"I would *die*," declared another.

And that was how Melody found herself slicked into her princessy place all over again.

She did not need to take stock of Prince Griffin to understand—merely from the elbow she held as he led her into the palace at a snail's pace—that he was kitted out much the same. The coat beneath her fingers had a luxuriant richness that seemed to meld with the hardness of his forearm. And if she listened, she could hear his military medals clink about on his lapel.

Her marriage might turn out to be fine. It was already better than she'd imagined, because Melody had never dreamed that she'd be left to her own devices. She never had been before. That was all good news.

But she worried that the studied formality of royal life might kill her.

"Do you always dress in formal clothes to visit your brother?" she asked as they moved into the part of the palace she recognized. The private royal apartments, where her sister now lived.

"Only when there is a photo opportunity," Griffin replied, and Melody found she liked his voice almost too much. It cast the same spell his physical presence did, as if there was a force field that emanated from it—from him—and surrounded the both of them when he spoke to her that way. Low and dark. Inviting. "And when it comes to things like national holidays, you can be certain that there will always be a photo opportunity."

"I will make a note," Melody said, without thinking, because she was still caught up on his *voice*.

Because if she'd been thinking, she certainly wouldn't have used that tone. It was far too sharp and dry and revealing of her actual personality.

She could feel his gaze on her, measuring. Aware, perhaps, that there was more to her than the role she played.

And they couldn't have that. So Melody clung to him instead, letting out a breath on a shuddery sort of high-pitched sigh.

"I'm so terrified I'll do something wrong," she lied. She endeavored to sound as feeble as possible. "There's a reason my father has always preferred to keep me out of the public eye."

Griffin stopped moving, forcing her to stop, too. She instantly balanced evenly on her feet, before it occurred to her that perhaps she should be feeble in gait as well. So she made a small production of tripping into him, which accomplished what she wanted.

He caught her. Easily and swiftly. Then held her up with an arm wrapped carefully around her back.

Melody told herself she should have laughed at that. Or wanted to laugh.

Instead, she could feel her whole body hum in response to that coiled, whipcord strength of his. To the heat of his body making her feel overly warm, everywhere. To the fascinatingly foreign and relentlessly male length of his torso pressed against her.

Oh, my.

"You will not be locked away ever again," Griffin told her fiercely. "You are a royal princess of Idylla, Melody. And more important still, my wife. If any accommodations need to be made, I promise you, it will be the world who accommodates you this time."

And all she could do was stand there with her face tilted up to his, her mouth slightly ajar in astonishment. Possibly in more than astonishment, though she couldn't say she fully knew what *more* was.

She could feel the flush that started deep and low in her belly flood through her, heating her up everywhere else. She could even feel it splashed all over her face when she'd spent long years learning to control her expressions.

But however she looked—no doubt flustered beyond repair—it clearly worked for Griffin. Melody told herself that was all that mattered.

Because he took her hands in his, solicitously.

She assured herself that what she felt was delight that her display of feminine weakness was doing its good work. And not…a different sort of feminine weakness altogether.

"You are safe now," he told her. "I promise."

And the oddest thing happened.

Melody, who had not felt truly unsafe in too many years to count—no matter what her sister thought about her prospects—felt a warm and happy sort of glow burst into bloom inside her.

As if she had needed saving.

And more, as if the promises of a strange prince who had been as forced into this marriage as she was meant anything to her. When…how could they?

Griffin stood there for a moment, his big, hard hands making her infinitely capable ones feel small and delicate. Something that should have appalled her—but it didn't. It really didn't.

While she was still trying to sort that out, he led her down the hall, murmuring his greetings to various staff members and royal guards as he passed. All while Melody clung to him, told herself she wasn't shivering slightly in reaction, and tried to sort out what was happening inside of her.

There was something about Prince Griffin. He was so…male. So big, so strong. So determined to protect her whether she needed his protection or not.

Melody liked it.

She more than liked it.

Because not only was she filled with that

marvelous sense of warmth again, there was that other heat again. That electric invitation winding itself around and around inside of her, part of that shivering thing and more, too. It sank low in her belly and set up a kind of pulse, and she knew that was all about him. It was because of him.

Melody was used to cataloging every stray feeling that moved through her body. She had a highly developed sense of where she was in space and knew how to find her feet and her balance. She also knew how to connect to herself, and knew from discussions with her sister and Fen that this was a skill the sighted often ignored because they took visual cues as gospel. Melody preferred using all the senses available to her, not just one.

And still, she had never felt quite like this. Her thighs seemed to whisper to each other as she walked. Between her legs she felt…heavy. Damp. There was an odd kind of prickling sensation working its way all over her skin. Her breasts—packaged into what her staff had assured her was a charming royal blue something or other that brought out her eyes, oh, joy—felt swollen.

Even her own palm seemed to generate more heat than it should, there where she clung to his elbow.

Whatever this was, Melody thought, she wanted more of it.

And then, with no little pomp and circumstance on the part of the palace staff, they were ushered into the presence of the King and Queen of Idylla.

Melody would have charged straight in to Calista, but she felt her husband pause. And understood what he was about even as he did it. She heard his heels come together, and felt it as he began to execute the quick bow that protocol demanded upon greeting the monarch for the first time in a day.

Accordingly, she snapped out her own curtsy.

And would have felt deeply silly had she not heard her sister huff out what sounded a lot like a laugh.

"Congratulations, Griffin," Calista said. "You've changed my sister overnight when I would have said that was impossible. Apparently all it took was a quick royal marriage to make her the proper Idyllian aristocrat we always hoped was lurking in there."

"You know you prefer it when I'm feral," Melody replied airily. The way she would have if they were alone. But, of course, they were not alone, so she forced herself to make a simpering little noise as punctuation. "I only hope that I am not too embarrassingly improper now that our circumstances have changed so much."

Her sister laughed again at that, even as Griffin murmured something soothing, and then there were more staff members everywhere. An endless amount of arranging and rearranging of the two royal couples on this or that bit of furniture in what Griffin told her—without her asking, as if he was attempting to be attuned to her needs—was the King's private parlor.

Approximately twelve thousand supposedly candid photographs later, the staff retreated, tables of food were wheeled in and their real Boxing Day could commence.

But Melody found that she was less interested in opening gifts than usual, because given her preferences, she would have continued to explore the wonder that was Prince Griffin's muscular forearm.

"Are you all right?" Calista asked in an undertone, when the gift-giving had finished and there was nothing left but the eating. And then more eating. The royal brothers were off in the far corner of the room, talking to each other near the windows that let in the sea air, already warmer and sweeter than before. "Did anything happen last night?"

"Many things happened last night, Calista. I was bartered off to a playboy prince as a kind of Christmas offering to the nation. Perhaps you heard."

"I don't mean the wedding. It was a glorious ceremony, you know. Christmas lights everywhere and you shining in the middle of it all." She sighed a little. Happily, Melody thought. "I meant after that, when he took you home."

Melody liked the idea of shining brighter than Christmas. It seemed to connect with that new, shivery electricity she could still feel low in her belly. She wanted to press her hands against her own abdomen to feel it, the way she'd experimented with electric things when she'd been young. To feel that hum. That buzz.

Then the burn.

And now, because of Griffin, it was inside her.

Waiting, she thought.

"Are you asking if my husband hauled me back to my brand-new home and plundered his newly acquired bounty?" Melody asked her sister dryly. "I think you'll find he's entitled to do precisely that, according to ancient Idyllian law. Fen looked it up to make sure."

Calista gripped her wrist. "He didn't…?"

"Of course not."

Melody went to lounge back against the settee where they sat, but stopped quickly when the dress she was wearing made that entirely too uncomfortable. Not if she wanted to also breathe. So she stayed where she was, straight-backed and formal, and after a moment, thought that was just as well. Talking with Calista, it was too easy to forget herself. And she shouldn't assume Griffin wasn't paying attention.

There was more to him than he pretended there was. She could feel it.

She reminded herself to keep her voice low.

"If he'd tried I would have maimed him," she said cheerfully.

"I think it's easy to assume that you might act a certain way in a certain situation when you imagine it from a distance," Calista said carefully. "But then, when the situation actually arises in real life, it might prove to be far more overwhelming than you expect."

That got Melody's attention. "I'm now a little more worried about your wedding night."

"I know you can take care of yourself," her big sister said, in a fierce undertone. "I'm hoping you didn't have to, that's all. Griffin has never struck me as the kind of man who would take something that wasn't offered to him, but you never know, do you?"

Melody's experience with men had almost exclusively been with her father. As Griffin was nothing like Aristotle, praise the heavens, she had personally been struck by…that, really. What he wasn't. *Who* he wasn't.

When she instead considered who he *was*, everything went electric.

"He was a perfect gentleman," Melody told Calista, and didn't quite manage to keep the note of complaint out of her voice. "What did you expect, with me playing this role? He thinks I might blow away in the faintest breeze. He would have to literally be a monster to force himself upon a creature he believes is so fragile."

Beside her, her sister made a funny noise. "Do you sound…unhappy about that? Or have I had too much sugar?"

"He has no intention of touching me," Melody said, as if she was making a proclamation. A quiet proclamation. She listened for a moment, making sure she could hear the low rumble of two male voices, still far enough away from the couch where she and Calista sat that there was no chance she'd be overheard. "I asked how we would produce heirs if there was no touching, and he didn't seem concerned about bulking up his part of the line of succession."

"Good," Calista retorted. "You hardly know him. No reason to rush into anything. You have your entire marriage for that."

"I'm sure we'll develop a beautiful friendship," Melody muttered. "But to be honest, I'm really much more interested in sex."

She heard Calista choke. "Excellent news on that front, then. You happen to be married to perhaps the most sexually experienced man in the whole of Europe."

"Sad, then, that he has decided he will never insult me with his touch." Melody sighed. "I have graduated from my own, personal, lifelong convent at last to discover that I've been sent to carry on more of the same in Prince Griffin's private monastery. It doesn't really seem fair."

"Our parents' house is many things, but I wouldn't call it a *convent*."

"That is likely because you were allowed to leave it. As you wished. Without any fears that you might put off the neighbors with your imperfections."

There was a small silence, and Melody instantly felt guilty. It wasn't Calista's fault that her father was who he was or that he'd always treated Melody so appallingly. And yet she knew full well her sister felt somehow responsible for it. For *her*.

"That wasn't meant to be an attack," she said. "Just a statement of fact."

Calista coughed, delicately. "Well. The thing is, Griffin is a man."

"I'm aware of that." Melody frowned. "Wait. What do you mean, exactly?"

"I mean that you've been particularly adept at using your body since you were a kid. And not to generalize hideously about my new brother-in-law, but he has always freely admitted that he's drawn to women who know how to use their bodies. Just…in a different way than you're used to using it."

It took her a moment. "Seduce him, you mean."

"Why not?" Calista asked. Across the room, the male voices got louder. And began moving closer. Calista leaned closer to Melody, speaking quickly. "What do you have to lose? If he gets overly excited you can kill him with one hand. Why not take the opportunity to play?"

Why not, indeed? Melody asked herself later, when, filled with too many pastries, cakes, and squares of baklava oozing with honey, Griffin led her back to their new home.

"What do you normally do for Christmas

dinner?" she asked, when they arrived in his entry hall. *Their* entry hall, she corrected herself.

"Are you hungry?" He sounded amazed.

"Not in the least. But I will be. Later."

"Well. Typically I have a light supper before…" He cleared his throat. "But, of course, I have no plans to go out this evening. I would be delighted if you would join me for a meal."

"Wonderful," she replied, smiling up at him.

As if he'd handed her the heavens instead of agreeing to share a meal with her. One he would clearly not be cooking himself.

Not that it mattered. She was pleased all the same.

Though, then, it was nothing short of torturous to allow him to carefully lead her back to her suite, clearly under the impression that she couldn't find her own way. And that even if she could, she was so breakable that she might crack into shards without his supervision.

There had been a great many years that she'd lain in her bed in her father's house as a girl, dreaming of one day being treated as if she was precious and perhaps fashioned from spun glass. Not a *princess*. But more the way Calista had been treated.

She wished she could go back in time and tell that girl how annoying it was.

"Thank you for a lovely Boxing Day, Melody," Griffin said in that marvelous voice of his that rumbled through her, collecting between her legs. "I am honored that I got to spend it with you."

Melody had the ridiculous urge to curtsy. And curtailed it. Barely.

"I am, too," she replied, laying it on a bit thick. In her opinion, she sounded more tearful than anything else.

"I will see you this evening, then," he said, in that rich, heady way of his.

"Yes," she whispered.

Melody slipped into her suite, then stood there, her back to the door she closed behind her. She heard the sound of Griffin's steps receding down the corridor. And then, moments later, the faint brush of a footstep at the end of her own entry hall.

Fen.

"Have you ever seduced a man?" she asked her sensei.

"Naturally," Fen replied, sounding unfazed.

Because Fen was always unfazed.

"You need to teach me how," Melody said. Because Fen was her sensei, yes, but she had also long been Melody's partner in crime when it came to quietly, secretly, making the embarrassing scandal of the Skyros family into a whole lot more then met the eye.

Pun intended.

"Very well, then," Fen said in her usual way, stern and sedate at once. "We have work to do."

CHAPTER FOUR

LATER THAT EVENING, Griffin waited for his
bride with his back to the cozy, intimate din-
ing area he'd had his staff prepare with this
holiday supper he'd told her was his tradition.
They'd run with it, festooning the room with
evergreen boughs that made the air smell
crisp and sweet, and small, twinkling lights
better suited to more northern climates.

The truth was, Griffin had no such tradition.

Historically, Boxing Day was what he considered the finish line of the deeply tedious
run of holiday balls that characterized the
last bit of each year. It was an Idyllian tradition. Every week, another holiday ball. All of
which he, as a royal prince, was expected to
attend. For years he had performed this duty
at his father, who had stopped asking Griffin to do anything—because Griffin would
refuse him. On principle.

But he would happily walk over burning embers for his brother.

It often felt as if he had, come Christmas. The good news was, after his final command appearance for the traditional Boxing Day photos the palace liked to release, he was free to do as he liked until New Year's Eve.

And what Griffin liked usually involved rounds of debauchery to balance out so many weeks of tedious duty and responsibility.

There would be no more of that, obviously. That was the promise he'd made.

That was the promise he would keep.

Griffin might have felt a faint pang at that, but he ignored it. He gazed out toward the sea instead. His residence sat up on the same hill with the rest of the palace complex and, on clear days, offered him sweeping views of whitewashed buildings with the Aegean forever beckoning in the distance. Tonight there were only the bright lights of the island's only real city and the brooding dark of the sea beyond.

A match for the brooding dark within him—but he was ridding himself of that, too. Griffin had been so many versions of himself in this life already. A doting son to a fragile mother. A rebellious son to a despised father.

An avid student, a clever soldier, a playboy prince. What was one more role?

A protector, this time.

This time Griffin intended to get it right.

He heard a sound behind him as the door was opened and his bride was led inside. *His bride*. His *wife*.

Griffin still wasn't used to those terms, but when he turned to face her, he forgot whatever pangs he might have had for careless nights with reckless people. Because Melody seemed to blot out any memories he might have had. Simply by entering the room.

He imagined that if it was daylight, she might block out the sun.

"I hope I'm not dressed inappropriately," she said in that breathy voice that made him want to conquer dragons and raze cities on her behalf. With his own two hands.

Melody looked frail and uncertain as she clung to the arm of her aide. The other woman was dressed all in black and held herself still in a manner that poked at him. *Too still*, something in him warned, as if he was still in the military. The aide was of indeterminate age and bowed slightly at the sight of him. Very slightly. And she did not smile.

But he dismissed that odd, poking feeling, because he was far more consumed with Melody.

"The staff who dressed me claimed that you'd said it was casual, but I don't know what casual means in a royal palace—"

"You look beautiful, Melody," Griffin assured her.

It was a throwaway remark. He would have said it to anyone so jittery and overwhelmed in his presence.

But in her case, he found he meant it.

Profoundly.

Gone was the pretty dress she'd worn earlier and the careful hair, fixed *just so* to look splendidly effortless in photos. Tonight, she wore what passed for casual in his circles. What looked like a whisper soft cashmere sweater over elegant trousers in a lustrous black. Her hair was down, but not in the wild way he'd seen it once before. It looked silky and smooth, and he had the near ungovernable urge to get his hands in it. To hold all that sunshine and gold in his palms and watch it slip through his fingers.

He tried to shove that unhelpful urge away.

"Do you require your aide's assistance to eat?" he asked.

Courteously, he thought. And yet he could have sworn that both of the women's expressions...changed. Tightened, almost.

"She can manage," the older woman said.

A bit forbiddingly, to Griffin's mind. Then, not waiting to be dismissed as she technically should have, she bowed her way out of his presence. And the room.

When the door closed behind her aide, Melody took a step—

And Griffin cursed himself for not moving sooner as he sprang across the room to take hold of her arm.

"We don't want you to trip, Melody," he said, as gently as he could.

"You are too kind," she replied.

Sweetly.

Too sweetly, something in him muttered, but he ignored that, too. How could his frail and breakable bride be *too* sweet when she could barely function without assistance?

He steered her, not to the table waiting for them, but out to the balcony where torches flickered against the December darkness.

"I thought it would be nice to sit outside tonight," he said stiffly. Because his wife was the only woman he'd ever met who he didn't instinctively know how to charm, and that was a prickly sort of realization. He didn't care for it. "We can have a glass of wine before we eat, if that appeals."

"That sounds like a wonderful idea,"

Melody said in her soft, gentle way. "I love torches."

Griffin paused in the act of helping her to the balcony's casual, comfortable seating area. "How do you…?"

And then watched, thunderstruck, as she laughed.

Silvery, like the moon. Like starlight.

"I can smell them," she told him. "And if you listen closely, you can hear the flames flicker in the wind."

But he was too busy questioning why his heart was galloping around his chest when all she'd done was laugh. *At* him.

He busied himself pouring out two glasses of the wine he'd requested from his cellars, then he went back to sit with her. There on the same comfortable bench near the torches that it had never occurred to him to listen to. Or smell.

Though he did then. And imagined he always would, now.

"I want to ask you a favor," his wife said after a moment, during which time he absolutely did not study the way she pressed her wineglass to that full lower lip of hers, slow and sensual.

"Anything," he said.

Hoping he sounded gallant instead of…obsessed.

Melody smiled, looking pleased. "My sister described you to me a long time ago. Your features, I mean. Calista told me all the girls swooned over the Royal Princes and she made sure I knew what you two looked like so I could swoon along with the best of them."

"And did you?" Once again, he found that when he was close to her it was difficult to recall why, exactly, he couldn't treat her the way he would any other beautiful woman. "Swoon. Over me. If you swooned over Orion, you're welcome to keep that to yourself."

"I was never one for swooning." She smiled after she said it, and he instantly forgot that oddly brisk note in her voice he'd thought he heard. "That was a very long time ago, though. And now we're married."

"Indeed we are."

"This time," she said, her voice hardly more than a whisper. So soft he had to angle himself closer to her to make sure he heard her. "This time I want to see you for myself."

She leaned in as she spoke, making him wonder why he'd chosen to torture himself like this, by sitting in close range. And then forgetting he'd ever questioned such a thing, because the scent of her swirled around him...and bludgeoned him.

Melody smelled sharp and sweet. Tart apples and brown sugar. And it took more self-control than Griffin thought he'd ever employed in his life to keep his hands to himself.

Though he couldn't seem to do much about his body's reaction.

"You can do anything you like," he managed to say when he was reasonably certain he could sound like something other than a slavering beast. "But I'll confess I don't know quite what you mean."

She smiled, her eyes so blue, that it was hard to believe she couldn't see him already. When he felt so *obvious*. He, who had never been any such thing in his life. He, who had made a career out of sampling any morsel that crossed his path, always letting them down so easily that they tended to trail about after him ever after. He, who had never been *obvious* because, it occurred to him, he hadn't really felt much one way or the other.

Before.

Who could have guessed that wanting something he couldn't have would *burn* like this? Brighter than the dancing flames that surrounded them?

And he tried to ignore the deeply male part of him that, because she was burned so brightly into his head, wanted to be the same for her.

God, the way he *wanted* the one woman he should have desired only to place behind protective glass.

Griffin was forced to acknowledge that he was far more like his father, the degenerate King Max, than he had ever wanted to admit.

Melody lifted one of her graceful hands off of her wineglass, then held it between them with her palm facing him.

"This is how I see." Her head tilted to one side, sending her hair cascading over her shoulder and that scent of hers dancing all around him. Griffin breathed in, deep, like he wanted to drown himself in her. He did. "Do you mind?"

His throat was tight. And he was harder than he thought he'd ever been. His sex was ready. *He* was ready. He could feel the pulse of his need, deep and low and insistent.

He should have been ashamed.

Yet he was…not.

"I would be delighted," he managed to get out, in a gravelly voice that no doubt betrayed him.

But he couldn't think of things like shame.

Not when Melody was leaning closer. Shifting her body so that her thigh was pressed against his. Torturing him—

"Would you hold this?" she asked, in that same soft, sweet voice.

Reminding him who she was.

And who, by contrast, *he* was.

Griffin took her wineglass from her. He ordered the beast in him back to its cage. And recited the promises he'd made—to his brother, to this woman, to himself—like a prayer as he gripped both glasses. Much too tightly.

Not that he expected prayers to help him. Not after the sins he'd committed—and gleefully.

Then he watched, transfixed, as she lifted her hands and carefully fit them to either side of his face.

The shock of it was like a blow.

He felt his pulse gallop. She was touching him, her hands cool against his jaw, while he could do nothing but burn. Her face was close to his, and that was another kind of heat. The scent of her filled his senses. Her hair, her skin, the soft curves in her lean frame.

But he didn't move. He didn't dare.

She moved her head as if she was listening

to something far away. A faint frown line appeared between her brows.

Griffin died a thousand deaths, yet somehow—*somehow*—kept his hands to himself.

And slowly, almost reverently, Melody began to move her hands as if he was made of Braille and she was reading every word.

Griffin had seen every possible sexy thing there was. He'd had them acted out upon him and acted them out in return. Yet he had never in his life seen anything sexier than this.

Than her.

Princess Melody, his bride, focusing on him with such intensity that he was sure if he squinted he would be able to see the force of all that concentration in a shimmering, electric arc between them. As if every light touch of her graceful fingers against his jaw, his cheekbones, the bridge and then the line of his nose, spread light.

She traced his eyebrows and his temples. She smoothed her fingers through his hair as if she'd read his mind and knew what he longed to do with hers. She found his mouth and traced her fingertips over his lips, seemingly heedless of the greedy flare of heat that kicked up inside him.

He shoved it back down. Or he tried.

Melody shifted beside him, and he couldn't

decide if it was a blessing or a curse that he was still holding on to both of their wineglasses. Surely it was a curse that he couldn't put his hands on her as she performed this oddly hushed and seemingly sacred act.

That was the blessing, too, he knew.

Because she was looking at him, that was all. She wasn't trying to seduce him. And in return, he wanted to devour her.

Melody didn't stop at his face. Almost dreamily, her hands drifted down to learn the column of his neck, that betraying pulse, and the width of his shoulders. He wore only a light sweater himself and found he missed the faint abrasion of her fingertips against his bare skin. She learned every muscle in each of his arms, then moved back to his chest. Her brow still furrowed, she used the whole of each palm to trace his pectoral muscles, then the ridged abdomen below.

And then slowly, with that same fierce look of concentration that had him hard enough to burst, she climbed her way back up again for one last pass.

Her face was so close to his. It was unbearable. And Melody moved a hand as if she knew what she was doing. As if she was deliberately positioning her palm she could pull his head to hers—

But she didn't.

It was an agony. He was *in agony.*

She stopped, her lips a scant centimeter from his—

"Thank you," she said, her voice that soft wisp of sound.

He barely heard it over the thundering inside of him. The clenching, near-unmanageable need.

"Melody…" Griffin began, though he had no idea what he planned to say.

Or if instead he might beg.

He, who had never begged because there had never been a need. Because he had never, in all his life, had occasion to want.

Not when everything was provided to him on a procession of silver platters. Not when any need or desire was met before he bothered to express it.

Griffin couldn't identify, at first, the thing that swelled in him when she dropped her hand. Then sat back, moving away from him, letting the December night back in between them.

Longing, he thought. *This is* longing.

In something that might have been astonishment, had it been less… bright.

Her smile made the stars seem like diamonds made of paste. "Now we see each other."

"You can see me anytime you like," he told her, and he was appalled by the sound of his own voice. His need so naked, so unmistakable, that he was surprised his shy and sheltered bride didn't recoil.

Griffin pressed her wineglass back into her hand, waited until she gripped it, then stood.

Deeply glad she couldn't see him wince as the heaviness of his sex…protested.

He moved to the balcony rail, entirely too aware that he was reacting as if she'd attacked him.

How he wished she would.

"I can't imagine what it is to be blind," he said then. Formally. Because he thought he ought to say something, if only to cover his reaction to her. "I'm sorry."

"I don't know what it is to see," Melody replied, smiling. "I can't accept your apology when I never lost my sight. I suppose I could sit about mourning something I never had, but what would be the point?"

"That sounds very healthy, Melody. I admire you."

"Do you? Why?"

It was possible that all that unfamiliar longing and need charging around inside of him was making him see things that weren't there, but for a bizarre moment, Griffin could have sworn that she was…issuing him a challenge.

There was something in the way she was sitting there, holding herself so still. There was something about the way her face tipped toward his, an expression he couldn't possibly be reading correctly on her lovely, innocent, guileless face.

Almost as if she was preparing herself to take some kind of swing—

But that was absurd.

This women needed his protection. She couldn't challenge a stray summer breeze, much less a man who still trained at military fitness levels to keep himself in fighting shape.

What Griffin needed to do, he acknowledged with a certain grimness, was accept the fact that his body was a lustful thing that wanted to drag his bride down to his level so he need not keep all the promises he'd made.

Accept it, get rid of it, and move on.

"I admire any person who handles adversity with such equanimity," he said after a moment.

He needed to get a grip on himself.

Now.

This was not an opponent of some kind.

This was his fragile, virtuous, helpless bride. Who had not touched him because she'd *wanted* to set him on fire.

That was an unfortunate side effect.

One that should have embarrassed him, as it highlighted that despite the trappings of his overtly civilized life, at heart he was nothing but a beast. Nothing but greed straight through, a slave to his own passions, like the father he despised.

She had been trying to see him, not seduce him. He should have been disgusted at his own response.

No more, Griffin vowed to himself. Again.

And made himself go and take his seat once more because he, by God, would be the master of his own flesh.

Melody inclined her head, demurely enough to make him question ever seeing anything but that in the way she held herself. "And I admire you."

He laughed, lounging back because this felt like familiar ground. "What is there to admire? I'm afraid I'm concocted of silver spoons, hereditary fortunes, and an entire lifestyle I did nothing to earn."

"Yes, but who would truly wish to be a royal?" Her smile was so gentle there was no reason he should feel the sharp edge of it rake over him. "It might be a pretty prison cell, or so I hear. But it's still a prison cell, isn't it?"

"It is an honor to represent Idylla and support my brother in all his works," Griffin said by rote.

It wasn't that he didn't mean it. He did.

But that didn't mean there weren't...textures to the words that formed the boundaries of his life. The simplest words, he'd found, always had the greatest complications lurking right there in plain sight.

"Of course you do," Melody said. Still with that smile. "I was lucky to avoid the bulk of my father's attention, if Calista's experiences are anything to go by. Being his favorite came with its own price tag, there's no denying it. It's not hard to imagine what being Crown Prince to King Max must have entailed."

"Heavy lies the crown," Griffin replied, lightly enough. "Which is one reason I have always preferred to keep my own marvelous princely brow smooth and unencumbered."

Next to him, Melody shifted. And leaned in.

And Griffin was a connoisseur of women. They flocked about him and he had long taken pride in the fact that while he frequently and enthusiastically indulged, he truly enjoyed those indulgences. He didn't have a type. He didn't have hierarchies. He wasn't attempting to put notches on his bedpost or prove anything to anyone. He simply loved women and loved being with them, whatever that looked like.

Yet here, now, as Melody swayed closer to him as if she planned to kiss him at last, Griffin felt like an untried innocent. A chaste virgin without a shred of control.

He wanted his hands on her.

He *wanted* and he didn't have the slightest idea what to *do* with it.

Inside him, storms and fires swept this way and that. It was cataclysmic. It was *too much*—

Griffin was somehow out of his depth when he would have said that was impossible. And all Melody did was sway ever closer…

Her scent, her warmth, wrapped around him like a fist.

He could remember, too intensely, the perfunctory kiss he'd delivered at the altar. It had been little more than a brush of lips and yet it *burned in him*—

God help him, but he wanted a proper taste.

But when she was so close that not kissing her seemed like an offense, what Melody did instead of put him out of his misery was… lift her hand.

Then, unerringly, find his forehead.

She traced her way down his to the furrow between his brows.

"Not so smooth and unencumbered, I think," she murmured.

It took some thousand years or so for her words to penetrate the wild drumming of his heart, the matching beat in his sex. The wildfire inside him, wicked and raging.

Melody's smile was cool. Almost as if she knew. "Maybe all lives have their hardships, Griffin. Maybe crowns aren't required."

CHAPTER FIVE

MELODY WOKE UP the next morning in a confused, grumpy rush, because there were voices and commotion and she could tell from the state of her own sleepiness that it was much too early.

Much too early.

She had never been a morning person. One of the benefits of having spent most of her life shut away from the sort of people her father wished to impress—meaning, everyone—was that she could keep her own hours. And did.

"No time to waste!" came a voice that reminded her entirely too much of the governesses she and Calista had suffered through when they were young. Brisk and self-important, every last one of them. "There are already too many appointments for one day!"

Melody lay face down, enveloped in the deep embrace of the glorious featherbed piled high with soft linens and fluffy down, as befit a royal princess's bedchamber. She had never felt quite so pampered in her life and intended to lie about, enjoying it, for as long as she could.

She had not, as she sometimes liked to pretend on the few occasions she was allowed to interact with people outside her immediate family, been forced to sleep on a pallet on the floor in her parents' dungeon. Her father was cruel, her mother weak, certainly. But on the off chance that Melody might ever compare notes with any other member of the Idyllian aristocracy, they'd made certain that while her rooms were far away from the rest in the sprawling Skyros villa—lest her father find himself forced to come face-to-face with Melody against his will, which was to say, ever—the rooms were appropriately outfitted.

Also, they did not have a dungeon. Aristotle preferred to imprison his daughters in a more lasting cage of disdain, rage, and insult.

Melody's ascension to the palace was not exactly the rags-to-riches story all the papers were claiming it was. She'd laughed over all the local articles that had called her Cinderella after her sudden Christmas wedding, making her screen reader repeat it again and again. Still, fairy tale or not, Melody found the accommodations of her new life as a princess nothing short of splendid.

She did not want to crawl out of her bed. She did not even wish to turn over. Particularly not when she was—despite the enduring embrace of the glorious featherbed—not nearly as well rested as she would have liked.

That was what happened when a person went and played seduction games with Prince Griffin, ate entirely too much rich food, pretended that it was all in aid of celebrating the holiday—and then was forced to allow him to escort her back to her rooms when even she could feel that the hour was too late and the tension between them too intense.

She hadn't expected the intensity, she could admit.

And when she had finally made it into her rooms, she'd been forced to endure a lecture from Fen about her deficiencies as a seductress.

I could have seduced him ten times already, for all you know, she'd told the older woman.

If you had seduced him even once, you would be in his bed, not yours, Fen had retorted, her voice as pointed as one of her lightning-fast jabs.

"I am still sleeping," Melody announced

now, more to her pillow than to the new voice still bustling around her room. Slinging open the curtains and stoking the fire, if the obnoxious noises being made were any indication.

"I'm afraid not, Your Royal Highness." And it was amazing how the voice made Melody's new title into the sharp lash of something unpleasant, like a whip. "A private citizen might enjoy these days off between Boxing Day and the new year, but that is not the way of the palace."

Melody burrowed deeper into her covers, and did not offer to introduce the intruder to the way of the fist as she wanted to do with every cell in her body.

"No, thank you," she said, again, with her face half-buried in the pillow. "Go away."

She was drifting back into blessed sleep within seconds, settling even deeper into the sweet clutch of her marvelous bed—

Until the covers, impossibly, were ripped off of her body, exposing her to the still chilly air of the bedchamber.

Melody felt murderous.

She flipped over, prepared to leap up and attack the woman that she could sense hovering there at the end of the bed, clearly overly impressed with herself—as any fool might be when they did not understand the consequences of their actions—

But she remembered herself just in time.

Melody was not herself. Not here. Back at her parents' house, she'd been taking care of herself for years and was accordingly left alone. *Here* she was a fragile, cringing, trembling little thing who would not, for example, catapult herself out of the bed and kick the person standing at the foot of it in the face.

She made herself breathe until the urge to attack faded. Then she shoved the great mass of her hair back and tried to school her expression into something appropriately deferential.

"I don't know who you are," she said quietly, yet with perhaps too much fury lingering there in her voice. She cleared her throat. "But you should know that I take my sleep very seriously."

"I am Madame Constantinople Dupree," came the voice once again, redolent with self-satisfaction. "I'm the foremost expert on courtly manners in the whole of Europe and have been gifted to you, Your Royal Highness, by His Royal Majesty King Orion himself."

"A gift for the girl who has everything," Melody murmured.

Not as nicely as she should have.

"I am led to understand that your manners are above reproach, which I will take the liberty to doubt, as I have never taught you."

"I did manage to marry a prince," Melody countered, and had to order herself to release the tension in her body, because this was no time to be wound like a spring, ready to attack. It would get her nowhere.

No matter how satisfying it might have been.

Madame Constantinople Dupree sniffed with pointed disdain. "A prince is but a man, Your Royal Highness. And it is not the men of society you need concern yourself with on your first day of social calls. You should be so lucky! Alas, it is the aristocratic women who will be coming to vet you today, I am afraid."

"Are you?" Melody shrugged before she thought better of it, and tried to pull off a bit of a cringe at the end of it. "I am not afraid of a collection of silly women who speak of nothing but last night's parties."

"You should be," Madame retorted with another sniff. "Believe me when I tell you that even if they have not sampled Prince Griffin's legendary charm personally, there will be no reason whatsoever for them to go easy on you."

"Save that I outrank them."

In return to what she'd thought was a winning argument by any measure, Melody heard a light, brittle sort of laugh. It reminded her so much of the sort of sound she'd been letting out herself since her wedding that she was forced to take more notice than she might have otherwise.

"My dear child." And she could hear things she didn't want in the other woman's voice, then. A seriousness. And an underlying bedrock of certainty. "Society's most fearsome women are coming to pay their respects to a new member of the royal family. Which you should be aware means they would love nothing more than to pick clean your bones, slay you alive, and destroy your reputation. Preferably over a lovely cream tea, with a charming smile attached. Never, ever underestimate the ruthlessness of a woman who seemingly speaks of nothing. She is almost certainly deliberately hiding her power, and a hidden power is nearly always far more dangerous."

Melody sat a bit straighter at that, for she knew it to be true of herself. Why not the great many aristocratic ladies she had never bothered to study, thinking them anything but worthy opponents? She should have known better after witnessing her sister's struggles over the years. Not all fights used the weapons she'd been training with for a lifetime.

But that didn't mean Melody intended to lose.

"It can't be that bad, can it?" she asked. "A bit of palace intrigue, perhaps? A few salacious rumors?"

"Whatever you are imagining, Your Royal Highness," replied Madame Constantinople Dupree, severely, "it will be worse. Much worse. And yet here you are, still abed in your nightgown, when we ought to be preparing you for war."

"War?" That sounded a lot more fun than the day Melody had imagined, but she reminded herself to shrivel a bit, like a frightened creature might. "I don't know…"

The other woman sighed. "They told me you were a frail, fragile little thing. Rest assured, that can only work in your favor. But we must act now."

"Very well, then," Melody said, with exaggerated bravery. And was certain she could hear Fen's snort of laughter from the hall. "War it is."

Accordingly, she surrendered herself to the brisk morning schedule outlined by Madame, who did not pretend to be anything less than a humorless drill sergeant. She allowed herself to be marched off to the shower, then whisked into the chair that she'd discovered during her explorations last night, sat before a vanity table. Inaptly named for a blind woman, perhaps, who could be vain in all manner of ways that did not involve mirrors, but she doubted that Madame Constantinople Dupree would find such commentary amusing.

As she sat there, letting servants buzz around her, breakfast was brought to her. And Melody was deeply unimpressed to discover it was little more than a hard roll to go along with her coffee.

"I prefer my breakfasts not to suggest that I might have woken up to find myself incarcerated," Melody muttered. To Fen, who had brought her the tray and who was currently pretending she didn't speak the local language—one of her preferred places to hide herself in the presence of others. None of whom, apparently, ever bothered to discover that she was, in fact, an Idyllian native. "Though I think they serve better food in jail."

"You may have as luxurious a breakfast as you wish, Your Royal Highness," Madame said in a forbidding tone from somewhere behind Melody. Once again wielding Melody's new title like a sword. "But I should warn you that you will be eating all day."

"That's the first thing you've said about the day ahead of me that sounds the least bit enjoyable," Melody retorted, because she hadn't yet had enough coffee to think better of it.

"Nothing about today will be enjoyable," came the swift, brisk reply. "You will be judged on what you eat along with everything else. How you sit. How you respond. How you laugh. How you hold your hands. You must view today as a comprehensive exam, Your Royal Highness. One from which it is extremely likely that you will emerge with dire marks from all involved."

"Will all these ladies pelt me with their tea sandwiches?" Melody asked dryly. Too dryly, she understood, when Fen refilled her coffee without her having to ask. "Sling pots of clotted cream at my head?"

It was difficult to pay attention to things like the expression she ought to have had on her face, or the tremulous tone she ought to have been using, when her staff was careening all around her. They were troweling on cosmetics she had no way of knowing if she liked or not and doing acrobatic things with her hair, all while Madame stood behind her, radiating disapproval.

It was only Fen's cough, in fact, that reminded her to shift her body language into something that made sense for the character she was meant to be playing here. To round her shoulders and make herself small instead of entertaining little fantasies of what it might be like to bat away clotted cream weapons, and expose her real self to any soft, pampered, vicious society ladies who imagined they could bully her in some way.

That would be satisfying, but foolish. And not at all the strategy that she was supposed to be employing. By decree of the monarch himself, in case she'd forgotten.

"I understand that this seems silly to you," Madame was saying in a tone that made it clear she did not, in fact, understand. Or wish to understand. "You've led a very sheltered life, after all. Protected from the intricacies of life at court."

That was not how Melody would have described her life, but she told herself to let that go. If anything, she should have been amused that after being considered the great, humiliating scandal of the Skyros family—something that couldn't be true, by definition, if she was now a member of the royal family and sister to the new Queen—there was already a new, usable fiction to explain why it was that she had been so seldom seen or heard from her whole life.

"Yes," she murmured, striving to sound overwhelmed rather than entertained. "Very sheltered."

"In a perfect world, I would have had months to prepare you," Madame said, reprovingly. "Years. Instead, I have but hours." She sighed. Heavily. "We will do the best we can."

"It is just…" Melody paused, because the woman tugging on her hair did something that made her eyes water. She blew out a breath as if that was emotion, not a sting. "The Prince did not say anything about this. He didn't even tell me there was anything for me to do today."

That was true, of course. But it was also true that she'd said it that way deliberately, to encourage them all to believe that she enjoyed a great intimacy with the husband she barely knew. The sort a newlywed bride ought to enjoy.

The sort everyone would assume she enjoyed, in all senses of the term, because it was Griffin.

"Prince Griffin enjoys the affection of the nation," Madame said with another helping of that severity. "He has spent a lifetime cultivating the goodwill of his people. He also enjoys the advantage of having been born royal. None of these advantages are yours, if you will forgive me."

Melody smiled demurely. "Of course. I am cognizant of my own deficiencies. How could I not be?"

But the joke was on her, because Madame did not rush to assure her that she was in no way deficient, the way regular, sighted people normally did in the face of any direct or indirect reference to her blindness.

"I'm glad to hear it," the older woman said instead. Stoutly. Forcing Melody to respect her, despite herself. "What you can expect are packs of hyenas, parading about as if they truly wish you might become friends one day. They do not wish this. You will be given no benefit of any doubt. You will be accorded zero room to maneuver or grow. They will come in prepared to eviscerate you. And will take pleasure in the fact that they might do so to your face, without you any the wiser."

For the first time, Melody felt something inside her…shift. The way it did when she was preparing herself to step into the ring. To fight with Fen, who never gave her any quarter.

"I am not as unaware of what goes on

around me as people might imagine," she said quietly.

"I am thrilled," Madame replied. "This is the first cause for optimism I have had since I entered your bedchamber."

And hours later, when Madame was cautiously optimistic but in no way satisfied, she ushered Melody from her own apartments to a set of rooms she and Fen had explored on her wedding night. Her formal reception rooms, she was told today.

For her sins.

"You have forty-five minutes before your first guest," Madame said briskly. "Is that enough time?"

"For what?"

Melody felt deeply grateful that she'd spent the bulk of her life studying the things she had. With Fen, who had never allowed her the luxury of self-pity. Because she could not imagine, otherwise, how she would have handled the morning she'd had. Madame was not a martial artist. But she was a sensei all the same, and had somehow managed to instill in Melody a deep appreciation for the finer nuances of snooty aristocratic behavior that she'd never before possessed.

It will not be enough to play the innocent, she'd said gravely. And more than once.

But I am innocent, Melody had replied.

Evenly at first. Then, as the hours dragged by, with far less equanimity.

Innocence is blood in the water, Madame had retorted. *Do not fool yourself on that score. You will find it is preferable to out-swim the sharks than to hope they are taken aback by innocence.*

Madame threw open the doors to the reception room and ushered Melody inside, Fen walking silently behind her.

"You must use this time to familiarize yourself with this room. I assume from the way you moved around your bedchamber and the rest of your apartments that you have a system for doing so. The more comfortable you are, the less ammunition you will give your enemies. Do you understand me?"

"Completely," Melody replied.

She and Fen used their forty-five minutes wisely.

And by the time Madame returned, announcing that the onslaught was to begin, Melody was as primed as if she was preparing to grapple.

Which was good, because grapple she did.

They came at her in order of rank. Something Melody had deliberately not concerned herself with in all her days, because what was the point, though she had received quite a crash course on Idyllian nobility today.

It was a parade of ladies with various titles, all of which they waved about them like taunts. Some were kind. Some pretended to be kind. Still others engaged in actual taunts, as if they did not expect that Prince Griffin's unexpected bride would be capable of telling the difference.

Melody could tell which ones had sampled her husband. Which ones had only wished they might. And which still intended to get their claws into him, despite his marriage.

She supposed another woman might dislike knowing such things.

But not Melody.

The more these women showed themselves to her, thinking she couldn't see who they really were, the more power she had over them.

"I cannot imagine how overwhelmed you must feel," cooed an openly poisonous member of the lesser aristocracy. Married to a minor lord, she nonetheless carried herself as if she had the consequence of a queen. *The* Queen.

From this, Melody was given to understand two things. First, that Lady Breanna was very beautiful. Second, that Breanna was not happy to discover that Melody was not disfigured, as some had liked to whisper to explain her absence from public events over the years.

Expectations were power, too, if a person knew how to use them. Melody did.

"How lovely of you to worry about me," Melody replied sweetly. "But there is no need for concern. I like to think that I've been training my whole life to step into this role."

"It appears that the Skyros family took their *education* far more seriously than some," came the arch reply. "I assume there were more opportunities to…ah, *study* than the rest of us were accorded."

Even if Melody had not received a morning-long crash course in how to handle just that sort of elegant poison masquerading as a conversation, she would have known that she was being attacked.

"Surely it is the role of any Idyllian citizen to support the royal family." She kept her voice friendly, as Madame had advised. Because it was always better to keep them guessing, the other woman had said. Making Fen guffaw, then pretend it was a cough. "That was how my sister and I were raised, in any event."

The only interest Aristotle Skyros had ever had in the royal family was how to rope the previous King into marrying off Orion. To Calista, so that Aristotle might therefore wield a greater influence over King and country. But that did not fit with Melody's performance here, of virtue masquerading as patriotism, all wrapped up in a shy smile.

"Indeed," trilled Lady Breanna. "As were we all. But I will confess, I don't think there's a soul on the island who is not *enchanted* to discover that Prince Griffin truly has the heart of gold we always suspected he did."

It was the same checklist that, by now, had been waved in front of Melody a thousand times today already. Her family was grasping and unworthy. She was out of her depth to a laughable degree. And, not least, Griffin himself had only condescended to stoop to taking a creature like *Melody Skyros* as his bride as an act of selfless charity.

Granted, that was all true. Particularly the last, but that didn't mean Melody had to like the way these horrible women threw it in her face.

Each and every one of them. With glee.

She leaned in. "I'm not sure he was thinking with his *heart*, Lady Breanna." She could feel the other woman's bristling outrage, so she decided she might as well stick the knife in. "I suspect it was a rather different organ altogether."

And it wasn't until the doors closed behind Lady Breanna and her sputtering indignation—likely because she had designs on Prince Griffin's organ herself—that Melody allowed herself a deeply inelegant cackle.

Madame would not approve.

The doors opened again and Melody tried to compose herself.

But she knew, almost instantly, that it wasn't another insipid well-bred lady come to offer her a raft of backhanded compliments.

She could feel the sheer male power, ruthless and intoxicating, like an abrupt change in temperature. It emanated from him, so that even if she hadn't heard the particular cadence of his steps—so familiar to her now—she would have known.

"Do not stop laughing on my account." Griffin's voice was low. Deep. Rough in a way that made her think of decidedly un-aristocratic things. And made her body hum in response, as if they were already doing them. "It makes you sound like a different woman altogether."

Melody knew she should have wilted. Curled into a soft little ball in need of his care, the way she was supposed to do. But something in her rebelled.

Maybe it was all the hours she'd spent today playing princess games. Maybe it was Griffin himself, bringing all that brooding, storming *maleness* in with him as he flung himself onto what she knew was a frilly, feminine little settee across from her.

She tried to imagine that. A man like him, so big, so hard, so deliciously male, overpowering that frilly piece of furniture without even trying.

A shudder seemed to come from deep inside her, wrecking her.

Or it would have wrecked her, she corrected herself. But she couldn't be wrecked. Not by hours of polite torture and not by him.

"As it happens," she said, because she couldn't resist, even when she knew she should have, "I believe I am a different woman, Your Royal Highness. I've been required to sit here for hours, smiling merrily while all your ex-lovers lined up to make sure I knew the precise length and breadth of your…"

She paused, deliberately.

He went still.

Dangerously still, but her trouble was, she liked that.

"*Reputation*," Melody supplied, at last. Innocently. "Your reputation. And better still, how true it still is today."

CHAPTER SIX

FOR A MOMENT, Griffin was certain he hadn't heard her correctly.

Not when his Princess sat before him, looking as fresh and pure as if she had just that moment descended from the clouds above, harp in one hand and halo attached.

Melody was radiant. She had spent hours in a pit of venomous snakes, and yet she sat there before him looking sweet and virtuous and wholly unfazed.

Even as she spoke of his *reputation*.

He eyed her a little more closely. She was dressed in what might as well have been battle armor. Her wedding dress had been a glorious confection, a fairy tale in fabric. The casual sophistication of the night before was left to his memories—and the filthy, erotic dreams of her that had kept him up half the night, to his shame. But today's ensemble was deceptively simple. The elegance was in the details. Not trying too hard—which the more vicious would have used as reason enough to sniff about her—and not trying too little, either, which would have branded her as haughty by some and unfit for her position by others.

Even her hair managed to look effortless yet sophisticated at once. It was tamed and swept back from her face, highlighting the perfection of her aristocratic bone structure. Her makeup was subtle, and instead of dramatic jewelry to proclaim her position, she had only demure hints of sparkle at her ears and the hollow of her throat.

Then again, the ring he'd put on her hand spoke loudly enough.

And the dress she wore was a masterpiece. Griffin imagined that he would see a great many dresses cut precisely like this on the island's fashionable ladies within the next few months. It was perfectly feminine, yet authoritative. It announced not only the elevation of Melody's rank, but signaled her ease with her new role. It was both more than a shift and less than a gown, showing off the heartbreaking beauty of her form while remaining modest enough to win the approval of even the most ferocious society matron.

He found he was…proud.

"I should have prepared you for what would happen today," he said, and then stared down at his hand, astonished to find he was pressing it against his chest. Because something there…ached. "I apologize that I did not. If I am honest, it never occurred to me that they would force this protocol upon you. I assumed you were relaxing into your new role, in private."

He had also been far too busy frothing about in the grip of his own demons. Not that he planned to share that with his innocent bride.

Who seemed to *glow* at him. "I'm actually pleased you did not prepare me."

Melody sat with her legs together and her ankles demurely crossed, a vision of propriety. Her hands were folded in her lap, gracefully, and he found himself staring at them—remembering how it had felt to have those very hands all over him.

And the fire that had kept him up half the night surged back to life. Flames licked over him while all of that *want* tumbled through him, making him edgy with need.

Making him think he might burn to ash if he couldn't get *his* hands on *her*—

Griffin didn't know what he might have done then. And he would never know, because the staff was all around them, seamlessly clearing away one set of tea things and bringing another to take its place.

And Melody looked as if she was staring right at him with her eyes like the sea in summer, when, of course, she wasn't.

That thing in his chest unfurled and ached all the more.

"You should not be pleased," he told her, and only when he heard his own voice did he realize how tense he was. He ordered himself to find his way back to the charm he was known for. "We have been married less than two days and I have already failed you."

"Not at all," his bride told him, her voice far airier than his. "It was far more fun to do it blind."

For a moment, he could only stare at her. Slowly, Griffin blinked.

Then watched, while that ache in his chest hitched and turned into something far hotter, as she smiled.

Wickedly.

He had the lowering, white-hot notion that if they'd been truly alone in this room, he would have ignored the table between them and gotten his hands on her at last. He would have taken her, there and then, any way he could.

It was that wickedness in her lovely smile. It was the way it changed her. Altered her face, making her look almost as if…

But then she laughed again, and this time, she sounded as innocent as ever. As pure and good.

Untouchable, something in him complained.

When he had vowed to protect her, not defile her. She was goodness personified. She deserved more than…him.

"I shouldn't say things like that," Melody said brightly, then laughed again. A tinkling sort of laugh, like a bell, that made him think of the sorts of churches he never entered. Griffin tried to ignore the lick of flames inside him. He tried to shame himself for all this greed, but failed. "Madame Constantinople Dupree was very clear on this point. But she did tell me that a little bit of firmness, just the faintest hint, wouldn't go awry."

"They eat sweetness for breakfast," Griffin agreed, trying to shift to make himself comfortable. But she was still sitting there before him, looking every inch the Princess, and he was undone. And uncomfortable. "And regurgitate it as a scandal whenever possible."

"Then I already have a leg up," she said, almost merrily. "As, being your foremost work of charity, I'm already scandalous."

There was nothing specifically untrue about that statement. There were many reasons that Melody was the right choice for him, forcing him to keep the promises he'd made to his brother in more ways than one. Married, settled, scandal-free and bonus, yes, his choice of the hidden Skyros sister had instantly made him seem far better than he was.

There was absolutely no reason that should sit on him, a heavy weight he couldn't seem to dislodge.

"What you are," he said, with more temper than should have been involved, surely, "is my wife. A royal princess. Should anyone treat you as something less than that, whether or not your tone is something less than polite will be the least of their concerns."

Melody smiled and this time, sadly, without that wickedness. "Can you imagine? A royal prince charges forth to defend his wife from passive aggressive comments… I can see the papers now. It would cause a terrible ruckus and neither one of us would look good at the end of it, would we?"

He considered her for a moment, realizing that this was yet another version of his wife.

Every time he saw her, it was as if she was someone else.

If he was any kind of a man, that should probably not excite him as much as it did.

But he found her fascinating.

"I did not marry you to force you into society battles," he said, because though she sat there looking as if she was perfectly happy to let the silence between them drag on forever, he found he was not. "There are no winners. Only Pyrrhic victories if you're very lucky. And everyone walks away stained."

"Are you stained, then?"

Griffin was glad she couldn't see the bitter twist to his lips. "Unto my soul."

Melody inclined her head. "That sounds unpleasant. You must know that there are solutions to that problem."

"Are there indeed?" He could think of several things that would feel like solutions. To him, anyway. "And what would you know of stains—or society, for that matter?"

"Only that it is the women who bear the brunt of both," she corrected him softly. "Men are allowed to be stained, aren't they? It gives them a certain appeal. Women, by contrast, must make certain they are spotless and beyond reproach. Or appear so."

She sounded as if she was parroting a hymnal. "We are not so medieval in Idylla these days, Melody."

"Perhaps you are not, Your Royal Highness," she retorted. And once again, he was sure there was more to her than manners and innocence. It was that flash of something like temper. It was the hint of *more*—but no. He merely wanted her, that was all. He needed to get used to that novelty. "You can act as you please. And do. Had I been in any doubt on that score, a number of your admirers came here today for the express purpose of letting me know exactly how many stains your soul bears. But naturally I cannot behave in a similar manner."

"Because you are a married woman, Melody." He told himself that wasn't temper that worked its way over him. Through him. Griffin did not lose his temper—ever, and certainly not around women. "My wife, in case you forgot."

"I didn't forget." Her expression was polite. Mild, even. And if he wasn't mistaken, faintly amused. He had no idea what to do with that. Or with her. "I was only making a point."

She turned her head away from him then, and he had the odd sensation that he was watching her...change. Especially when she seemed to cower where she sat.

"I only hoped to…not embarrass you," she said in a wispy voice. "I'm sorry if I failed. My father could have told you that was inevitable."

Griffin told himself he should feel nothing but the urge to protect her. From the world. From her odious father. From himself.

But instead, what he wanted most was to touch her. To feel her beneath his hands. To see the truth of her the way she'd seen him—because he couldn't quite believe what he saw before him. He couldn't make sense of it. Of her.

If she was as frail and beset as she looked just now, how could she possibly have fended off the fangs of so many society women?

You only wish she was secretly strong and capable, a voice in him chided. *So you could stop pretending to be good.*

He cleared his throat. "I regret that you were put through that. I apologize if you found it an ordeal."

"You have a past. I understand that." She turned her face back toward him. "Should we pretend that you do not?"

He had been about to say something similar. And found he didn't like it much when it came out of her mouth.

"I would prefer that you not be confronted

with anything you find unpleasant," he managed to say.

"Goodness. I didn't realize that was on offer." Again, she smiled, and he began to understand how she'd held her own today. "I rather thought that this was a life we were going to have to lead, together. For who among us lives a life devoid of unpleasantness? Even in a palace?"

She should have been soft. Yielding. In tears.

That she was not seemed to lick its way beneath his skin. It...bothered him.

"I cannot tell if this is all a mask for your rage or if you truly are as unbothered as you seem," he said instead of addressing all those half-notions he was sure would sound like so much wishful thinking if he said them out loud.

His wife—his Princess, chosen for her fragility—smiled. And did not look in any way fragile. "I'm an open book."

"Perhaps. But not in any language I speak."

Her head tilted to one side. "Do you speak many languages, then?"

Was he relieved that she was changing the subject? Shouldn't he have been?

"I speak a great number of languages." Griffin shrugged that off even as he said it, because it was second nature to live down to any and all expectations. "I spend half my time conversing with dignitaries from various countries. It's easy to pick up a few things."

"And here I thought that conversing was not exactly your most notable people skill."

He thought he ought to apologize. But he'd already done that.

Her smile changed yet again. He found he was becoming obsessed with it. Soft and innocent when everything in him was wicked.

Or, like now, as if he entertained her.

"I don't begrudge you your past," Melody said. "Surely we can indulge each other in that."

"Do you have a great many lovers in your past, then?" he asked before he thought better of it.

Because the truth was, he was surprised to discover, that he did not feel indulgent on that topic.

At all.

Her smile seemed edgier, though he could have sworn nothing about it had changed. "It would be a sad life indeed without a few great loves scattered about."

Griffin opened his mouth to reply to that, but then stopped. He reminded himself that he was meant to be charming, for god's sake. "A great love could be a book. I think, somehow, that you would be less…whatever you are had you been faced with my library today."

"Is your library digitized? Because if not, I'm afraid, Your Royal Highness, that it's only a room to me."

"It is not digitized, no." Griffin was ashamed to realize he hadn't even thought about that. He pulled out his mobile and fired off a message to his chief aide. "But it will be."

"Wonderful," Melody said.

When he looked up from his mobile, she was lifting the teapot and pouring out tea for both of them, then replacing it, all with an ease of movement that would have convinced him that she couldn't possibly be blind if he didn't know otherwise. She picked up her tea, and sat back in her chair, sipping at it.

"Never fear," she said. Calmly. Softly. Because he was making things up in his head to cater to his sex. He knew that. "Whether you make your library accessible for me or not, I have no intention of parading a selection of lovers in front of you. I think we both know that would be frowned upon by every last citizen of the kingdom."

Innocent. Pleasantly intelligent. In no way the sort of wicked, fallen woman that he considered his real type. She deserved better than him, better than the man he really was. He had vowed to give her the Prince he ought to have been instead.

And he would do that, even if it killed him. He would.

"I am a man with a rich and complicated past," Griffin told her, because she ought to hear that from him as well as in the form of a thousand inevitable barbs from others. "If your past is also rich and complicated, I can hardly complain."

Something he had always believed in, as a matter of fact. Fervently.

But saying those words…hurt. It was like the syllables curdled his mouth.

"You are so progressive, so open-minded and modern," she murmured. And if it had been anyone but Melody, he would have been sure that note he heard in her voice was sarcasm. But she smiled at him, beatifically, and he tried to shake it off and accept that she was who she was supposed to be—not who he *wanted* her to be. "My great loves are not men. You have nothing to fear. I come before you untouched and virginal, because nothing will please the crowds more than a man of great experience with a woman of none. Is that not so?"

Griffin was becoming increasingly tired of the way she did that. Ripping the ground out from beneath him when he was used to being in control of his surroundings. Spinning the world around and around on its axis until he was dizzy. He studied her as he lounged there opposite her on an uncomfortably spindly piece of furniture that he suspected had been deliberately chosen to make the parade of overtly curious society ladies ache a bit as they flung their daggers at the new Princess.

What he didn't know was whether Melody herself was responsible for that sort of thing. Or if she was simply being guided, lamb to the slaughter, straight into the heart of the schemes and scandals of Idyllian society.

More than that, he couldn't tell which he wanted it to be. Did he want a fragile innocent who he truly believed would bring out the heretofore unknown decency in him? Or did he want what the fire in him wanted—a far more complicated creature, capable of defending herself from the onslaught of would-be rivals and all manner of wickedness with what looked like carefree ease?

He knew what he *should* want.

But that seemed to do absolutely nothing to cure the way his blood pumped hot. Or the erotic images that poured through his head the way they had last night, with the same results.

Griffin was burning alive.

"I'm afraid that your long day of torture will extend into the evening," he told her when he could speak. "We have an intimate dinner party to attend. And by intimate, I'm speaking in terms of the standards of the palace. Twenty people, or so. Thirty at the most."

"Just a few friends, then."

Was he smiling—a real smile? Extraordinary. "Never make the mistake of thinking that any of these people are your friends. Especially if it feels like they are."

He meant that as a throwaway remark. To go along with this surprisingly uncomfortable discussion. Because that's what it was, he admitted. That feeling clanging around inside him. It was pure, undiluted discomfort. He didn't like the idea of vipers like Lady Breanna—who he'd had the misfortune of seeing as she exited—sitting here and sniping at his bride.

Across from him, Melody tilted her head toward him in that way that made him feel more examined, more *visible*, than the regard of any other person he'd ever met.

"I had no idea," she said. As if she pitied him. Griffin wanted to run from the room, and that was so uncharacteristic it rooted him to the spot.

"About what?"

And he was not pleased that he sounded gruff. Bothered.

"I take loneliness for granted," Melody said quietly, and again, something…shifted.

They were sitting in the formal reception room of his residence. It was among the prettiest rooms in the whole of his house, which was not a mistake. It had been designed to let in the light and the sea, so anyone who entered felt instantly steeped in the glory of Idylla.

He certainly did. It was as if the sea and the sky surrounded her like a halo and lifted her up, making her something celestial.

Griffin had taken advantage of this room himself, upon occasion, but Melody somehow made it look natural. As if the room had been built specifically to showcase her glory.

And he did not think that it was a trick of the light that made the staff waiting against the wall seem to disappear. It was the huskiness of Melody's voice.

She sounded as if she was telling him a deep truth rarely spoken.

Griffin found he was very nearly holding

his breath. His heart pounded. He did not know what to *do* with himself.

"I don't mean to suggest that I didn't enjoy my childhood, because I did." Melody toyed with the delicate teacup in its saucer, held neatly in her lap. "Yes, my father was unpleasant, but as we've already established, life is not meant to be a parade of pleasantries. Still, I did not make friends the way my sister did. It was not encouraged. I grew used to my own company at an early age. But this cannot be a surprise. You know how I was raised."

"An insult that will be addressed," Griffin found himself saying, low and dark. "I promise you that."

He had the impression she was studying him, in her way. She sat so still. She seemed to be listening so intently he was sure she could hear that wild heartbeat of his.

"I imagine it's as easy to feel alone when your public life is relentless as it is when you are confined to solitude," she said after a moment. "It's just that no one thinks of it that way."

Griffin wanted to laugh that off. The way he would have at any other time.

But there was something about the way the air felt tight between them. There was the memory of her fingers moving over his face, making him feel naked. Still. The way she saw him, here and now, in a way that had nothing to do with the masks he wore for the world. The roles he played. The Prince Griffin he'd made into a performance.

"I grew accustomed to the contours and duties of my life long ago," he said. Stiffly. "I do not require sympathy for that. I'm well aware that my life is made up of great privilege. It should come as no surprise there are prices to pay for an accident of birth."

"You have gone to such lengths to pretend otherwise."

It wasn't an accusation. Griffin could have handled an accusation. He could have dealt with an undercurrent of dry wit or an arched brow. That would have put them back onto familiar ground. He would have known what to *do*.

Instead, he sat forward, and somehow managed not to reach across the narrow little table between them to take her hand. To toy with the ring he'd slid there himself.

"It is not that I was pretending," he told her, though she was a virtual stranger and no matter that he was married to her. "It was that Orion's role was always so clear. And I… had no wish to compete with him. It seemed easier not to try."

He had never said something like that before. Not out loud. Not to someone else.

Across from him, Melody leaned forward and put her tea back onto the table before her with a decisive *click*. She stayed like that, leaning forward. Closing the distance between them enough that if he'd only reached out, he could touch her at last.

He didn't.

Griffin had no idea how, but he didn't.

Even though the look on her face was so intense it made him imagine what it would be like to slide deep inside her. To claim her.

To know her the way she seemed, too easily, to know the parts of him he'd never let out in the light.

"What would happen if neither one of us pretended to be anything we were not?" Melody asked.

And the things Griffin yearned for then didn't make sense to him. It was as if they were someone else's dreams, but they starred him, and her, and not only in his bed. She made him want more than her body. She made him want *her*. And a whole life filled with the things other men deserved, but he never had. It was a violent, clattering thing inside him, loud and discordant.

That was what he told himself.

Because he hadn't been lying to her when he'd told her he'd never considered the issue of heirs. He'd never wanted any part of that mess, being a product of it himself.

Griffin didn't understand why, looking at this woman who should have been nothing to him but a kept promise, all those things that had never appealed to him before suddenly seemed...beautiful.

But in the next moment, he shook it off.

And laughed.

Loud enough to chase the clatter away.

"That seems a little one-sided," he said, relaxing into his seat as if it was comfortable. Because that was one of his talents—he could make himself relaxed and boneless anywhere. He excelled at it, in fact. "What could you possibly have to hide?"

And it wasn't until later that he would realize he recognized the look on her face then. It wasn't until later that he would put it into context.

She laughed, too, but only after a moment.

Only after she looked—for the briefest moment—as if he'd slapped her.

CHAPTER SEVEN

THE SO-CALLED INTIMATE dinner party was both boring and thrilling, which didn't surprise Melody in the least. Not after a lifetime of hearing Calista's stories about such gatherings. All that hostile gentility over the soup course, animosity disguised in airy chatter about nothing, and blood feuds concealed in manners so fine they squeaked.

"You appear to be enjoying yourself far too much," her sister murmured when the women repaired en masse to one of the salons, an archaic custom Calista had always claimed to enjoy as it permitted a glimpse at the real faces of women who preferred to act out characters in the presence of men.

"*Enjoy* is a strong word," Melody replied. She sat with her sister on one of the salon's many couches, thereby giving the rest of the women tacit permission to sit as well. "It's informative, isn't it, these awkward gatherings of so many soft creatures."

Calista made a reproving sort of sound. "They only appear soft, Melody. When it suits them. Beware the talons beneath."

Melody knew that she and her sister had very different definitions of softness. But as Calista shifted into her queenly hostess duties, Melody settled back against her seat and tried to exude it. She tried to look shy and fragile and all the rest of the things she was supposed to be—*soft* chief among them. She had already met most of the women who were now fluttering around Calista, jockeying for position and pretending their only goals were sudden, bosom friendships with the brand-new Queen. And while she found a measure of enjoyment in pretending she really hadn't noticed all the slings and arrows these same women had thrown at her in their private audiences earlier—and continued to throw out in their usual understated ways—she spent most of her time sitting softly at her sister's side. Fuming.

At herself.

She didn't know what had come over her this afternoon. She blamed it on back-to-back tea skirmishes with Idylla's viper class, which would surely make anyone loopy. That was the only reason she could think of to explain why she'd actually tried to *build a bridge* with Prince Griffin.

And had basically admitted to him that she was hiding things, though he hadn't picked up on it.

That didn't mean he wouldn't.

Melody could not pretend she knew her husband very well. How could she when she was acting a part herself? But she knew already that whatever else Griffin was, and whatever he might like to pretend in public, he was nowhere near as foolish as the tabloids liked to claim.

He was far too self-aware, for one thing.

And tonight, as she sat about attempting to look overset and trembly while surrounded by so many high-placed members of society—all of them chattering about nothing in particular while political and powerful undercurrents flowed as freely as the wine—Melody was forced to conclude that he was a whole lot more than that, too.

The way she had the day of their wedding when she'd first noticed that leashed power in him, such a surprise in a man who acted as if all he was, ever, was *charming*.

"You seem subdued," Griffin said when the dinner party finally ended and he was once again walking her slowly back through the palace. *Guiding* her as if, left to her own devices, she might topple over, hit the marble floors, and stay there until discovered. "I hope you didn't find the night too taxing."

Melody fought back a flash of irritation. *No,* she wanted to snap at him, *I do not feel overtaxed. I feel bored out of my skull.*

As anyone would, should they find themselves called upon to play a hapless ninny.

But she didn't say any of that, and not only because she had been asked to keep him in the dark—to keep him like this. The unlikely champion of the most inadvertently scandalous heiress in the kingdom.

"I was thinking about you, actually," Melody said instead.

Her hand gripped his elbow, so she could feel the kind of shock that went through him. It rippled in him, there beneath her fingers. She wanted, more than anything, to…lean in. To follow that shock, that reaction, and see where it went.

That was how she'd learned the shape of the world. She touched it. Traced it. Felt the heat of a thing, or its coldness. If it was hard or soft, pliable or unyielding. Fen had spent years guiding these explorations, explaining what figures of speech meant, and giving Melody touchstones.

But that wasn't how she wanted to touch Griffin. Not exactly.

She wanted to touch him to learn, certainly. Melody had not had the opportunity to touch many men. There was a novelty factor.

Still, she knew that mostly, she wanted to put her hands on him because touching him made her *feel things.* She wanted to explore it. She wanted all those things she'd read about and more, the opportunity to practice them the way she did her forms and strikes. Until there were no mysteries, only sensation.

But she supposed that even if she wasn't pretending to be someone she wasn't, that sort of thing would almost surely be frowned upon out in the halls of the palace. There was always protocol to consider—that and all the other things Madame Constantinople Dupree had banged on about this morning.

"You were thinking about me?" Griffin laughed, another thing Melody could feel vibrate through him. And through her. "That's a shallow pool, I think you'll find."

"That's what's so fascinating." He opened the door to the courtyard and led her through it, and something about the cool air on her face made her distinctly aware of how overheated she was. As if her body was taking in all those vibrations and sensations between them, charging her up, and making her glow with it. The way the lightbulbs she'd cupped as a child had, buzzing faintly until they grew too hot to hold. "I think everyone sitting at that table tonight actually believes that about you."

"I beg your pardon?"

He slowed, which shouldn't have been possible. As they were already nearly crawling. But for once, Melody didn't mind his deliberate, overly careful steps. She could feel the expanse of the courtyard all around them. And the density of the December air, pressing in. It made her feel as if the night was wrapped tight around them, threaded through with intermittent bursts of heat.

Not all of that from the evenly spaced heaters.

"I have no idea what they see, of course," she told him. "I assume you laugh and smile and do all the usual things with your face."

"The usual things…" he repeated, as if she'd said something shocking. "Forgive me, but how do you know what things people do with their faces?"

"How do you think?"

Melody laughed, but not because she was

amused. Not really. It was more like there was a steam rising in her and she had to let it out as if she was a kettle set to boil. And her own laugh, the faint and tinkling one she was allowed while she stayed true to her character, should have reminded her what was at stake here.

But she still lifted her free hand. And without questioning her motives—because she already knew perfectly well they were not the least bit pure, because she was not the character she was playing—she slid her palm over his mouth.

That sensual, firm mouth of his that made her whole body shiver into a kind of tight, hot awareness.

"Say my name," she told him.

A soft order, but an order all the same. After she said it, it occurred to her that perhaps this frail, wispy creature she was pretending she was would not be standing about issuing orders to a prince. But it was too late.

"Melody," Griffin said.

And she couldn't tell which made her feel more raw. The brush of his lips against her palm, making her dizzy. Or that note in his voice, a warning and yet something darker, something sweeter, at the same time.

"Now frown and say it," she said.

And Griffin complied, sending more sensation soaring through her, shooting out from her palm and finding all the places where she was the most feminine, the most entranced by him. Her breasts. Her belly. That slick heat between her legs.

Her voice hardly sounded like hers. "Once more, with a smile."

And that time, it was as if he said her name directly into the molten core of her.

Melody didn't know what to do with that kind of storm. That kind of need. The wallop of it that nearly took her knees out from under her—when she had learned how to balance while standing in the Aegean, either maintaining her connection to the shifting sands beneath her or getting tumbled by the waves.

This was far more difficult than that.

"Is that how you learned?" Griffin asked, his tempting, fascinating mouth brushing against her palm and sending impossible licks of flame spiraling into every part of her.

It took Melody longer than it should have to drop her hand.

"People's words sound different depending on what they're doing with their faces," she told him, unable to tell if she sounded fluttery or forthright because of the noise in her head. The pounding of her pulse and worse, the way it streaked all the way through her to lodge in the place she was softest. "And the more you listen for such things, the more you pick up on the subtleties. Calista and I used to hide in our parents' drawing room, where they would have their strange little parties that were almost always power trips of one sort or another. And afterward, we would parse everything we'd heard and everything she'd seen, so that I could get better at picking up on inflections. I got very good at it."

She could feel the weight of his stare, then. Probably because the trembling fawn of a charity princess she was meant to be would no doubt faint dead away before she'd indicate that she might have any skills at all. But there was no taking it back.

Deep down, she could admit, she didn't want to take it back.

You don't want his pity, do you? a snide voice inside her taunted her, sounding entirely too much like her father. *You little fool. You want the most famous Lothario in ten kingdoms to* admire *you.* You.

Melody could fight anything—except the obnoxious voices in her own head. But she could ignore them.

"I think you're the one who's fascinating, Melody," Griffin said, but there was that gallant note in his voice again. So carefully courteous that it bordered on condescending, to her mind. "To have achieved any of the things that you have strikes me as nothing short of a miracle."

Whatever, Gaston, she thought grumpily.

"It's not a miracle," she said, perhaps a little too crossly. "I didn't have a choice. The more blind I looked, the more it offended my father. It was simple math. The better I got at acting as if I had my sight, the easier it would be all around."

"And again." Griffin's voice was like a shudder in bones. "I do not intend to let that behavior on your father's part slide."

"My father has already been amply punished for his sins," Melody said impatiently. "In the only way he is likely to notice. He's lost his company. He's been cast out of the highest circles of power in the land. The daughter he attempted to control defied him, the daughter he preferred to ignore has been elevated to spite him. For my part, I would prefer to pretend as if I don't know he's alive. Repayment in kind, if you will."

"I had no idea you were so… cold."

Griffin sounded both as if he admired that and was confused by it.

Melody was straying off course, but she

couldn't seem to help herself. She could have corrected it then, before he had time to really think about how different she was acting. She could have toppled over into a swoon, or started cowering before him... But she couldn't quite bring herself to do any of those things.

This character she was playing was beginning to feel like a chokehold.

"Tonight, all those people sat there, thinking they knew you," she said instead, though she knew better than to indulge herself in this. Why couldn't she seem to stop? "I assume you must put on a good show. But I could hear you. I heard the way you directed the conversation—a perfect counterpoint to whatever your brother was saying. When you got loud, it was so he could speak quietly with whoever was nearest him. When you were outrageous, or entertaining, it was to allow him to continue discussions he didn't want the others overhearing. Quite a team, aren't you?"

Griffin had gone stiff again. "I made a vow long ago to serve my brother's interests as my own." His voice was made of steel, much like his arm. "We are all we have."

"I don't understand how the whole nation doesn't realize what a team you are. Instead, article after article witters on about how he is good and you are bad. Light and dark, day and night. As if you could have one without the other."

"Melody." And there was a different note in his voice then, something male and warm. She itched to put up her palm and *feel* the way he said it. "Are you...defending my honor? I must tell you, this is an exercise in futility at best."

"I vowed to honor you, did I not? There on an altar before the King and all the world. Surely defending that honor is implied."

"I like this fierceness in you, Princess." Griffin was shifting, reminding her that they'd stopped on their walk across the courtyard. That they were out in the night, the sea air batting at them, and still. Still, between them, this beguiling heat that was making her...foolish. "I like it very much."

His hands moved to grip her upper arms, and Melody knew well the language of *grips*. Holds and releases. The way that bodies moved together and apart, in an endless dance of forms that could be meditation in practice and violence on the street. She knew how to fall. How to fight. How to use every inch of her body as a weapon.

But this was...something else.

This was a melting, a melding.

She felt as if she was dissolving, as if the hard heat in his palms was changing the very composition of her body. As if it was streaking inside, and making her something different. Something new.

Something better, a new voice inside her whispered.

She could feel it—*him*—everywhere.

"Why do you feel you must hide?" she asked him.

He made a low sort of noise, as if she'd landed a gut punch. "I don't consider it hiding. Light and dark, day and night—these aren't insults. And it has always been easier, where there is already a bright sun, to become the moon instead."

"Does your brother know?" It was difficult to concentrate already. And when he began to move his thumbs up and down over her upper arms, almost absently... Well. Melody couldn't stop the goose bumps that rose everywhere he touched. Or the shiver that wound around and around inside her, showing no signs of stopping. "Or does he think what everyone else does—that his only brother is a committed degenerate like your father? Only, somehow, more popular than King Max ever was. As if by magic."

She should not be speaking to him like this. Melody knew she shouldn't. She owed her sister her loyalty, and by extension, her sister's husband. Calista wanted this marriage for Melody's sake, to keep her safe. Just as Melody wanted her own situation to be stable and her person protected well enough—not because she felt unsafe, but because it made Calista feel better. She understood all this.

More, she had agreed to all this.

But nothing had prepared her for the *heat*. Griffin's thumbs moved almost convulsively against her arms and that was the only thing she could seem to keep in her head.

"Do not mistake the matter." Griffin's voice was almost indistinguishable, then, from the night air that moved around them. But inside her, every word was almost too hot to bear. "I was reckless and heedless by choice. Hedonistic and no doubt remarkably asinine. I enjoyed my youth, Melody. And as long as my father was alive, there was no possibility that I could ever catch up to his level of seedy, irresponsible behavior. Just as there was no possibility that I could ever compete for Orion's halo."

"Why must there be catching up or competing?"

"I did not *pretend* to be badly behaved,

Melody," Griffin told her, as if the words stuck in his throat. "I *enjoyed* being badly behaved."

"Yes, yes," she said quietly. "You cut a swathe through the female population, sampling supermodels like candy. I know."

His grip tightened almost imperceptibly, but she felt it. And thrilled to it.

"I am beginning to find it concerning that you are the only citizen in the kingdom who has no problem whatsoever with my…appetites."

"Perhaps because I appear to be the only citizen in the country who also knows the rest of the story," Melody threw back at him, perhaps a bit recklessly. "However you might have fed those appetites, it was never at the expense of the palace. You never made yourself a liability—not even to your father, who certainly wouldn't have noticed."

She couldn't seem to *think* with his hands on her, skin to skin. It was too…encroaching. It seemed to get into everything, leaving nothing but flames behind.

"A happy accident," Griffin said, his voice a quiet warning. "Nothing more."

"I don't think so. I think you are far more in control of yourself and this reputation of yours than you wish to admit."

"That would be a true Idyllian scandal." Griffin's face was closer to hers, then. And the way he was gripping her, she had no option but to rise up on her toes. No option and no desire whatsoever to do anything but that. "And that cannot happen, Melody. No more scandals. My brother has decreed it."

He was so close, now, that she couldn't seem to keep herself from touching him. She ran her hands lightly over his chest, finding the lapels of the coat he wore, and better yet, his hard pectoral muscles beneath.

And inside herself, felt nothing but fire.

"Everybody knows that you married a charity case like me to make yourself look like a good man," she said. "To medicate against the possibility of any scandal, ever. They took pleasure in telling me so today, over and over again."

"If I can give you any piece of advice, Princess, it would be this. Never listen to the opinions of snakes. Especially when you have not solicited them."

"But that's not the real truth, is it?" Her voice was a whisper, at odds with the crash and burn inside her, her pounding heart, the giddy rush of her blood. "The real truth is that, deep down, you've always been a good man."

"You are sweet and naive," he growled at her, and she could *feel* his words against her own lips. "Innocent and almost unimaginably vulnerable. Especially here, in this palace of games and pretenses."

Melody wanted to show him exactly how wrong he was about that, but somehow, she couldn't seem to move. As if he was in control of her body, not her.

Something that should have alarmed her. When instead it made her...lightheaded.

"But beyond all of that," Griffin kept on, his voice laced with heat just like she was, and something like greed, "you're also wrong. You have no idea the things I want to do to you."

"Then do them," Melody managed to say. "I dare you."

"Careful what you wish for, wife."

There was too much heat and noise inside her, making her limbs feel heavy. She felt sluggish. And yet, at the same time, hectic.

It was as if she had a sudden fever. She even felt weak.

But not, she understood in the next moment, in any way ill.

And there would never be a better time than this. So much for attempting seduction, she thought. Fen was right. She was terrible at it. It was high time she tried a more direct approach.

Following an urge so overwhelming it hurt, Melody closed that last, scant bit of space between them and pressed her lips to his.

She remembered their perfunctory kiss at the altar. She'd had the impression of firmness, maleness, but that was all.

This was different.

Griffin went still. Radically still.

And she could feel the heat in him, all that marvelous, leashed power, while he held himself back as if he was afraid of hurting her. Or overwhelming her.

Melody, on the other hand, was not afraid at all.

She slid her hands up to loop them around the strong column of his neck.

And then…she played.

Once, when she'd been a teenager, she'd kissed one of the statues that lined the atrium in her father's house. Because it was shaped like a man, and Calista had told her about kissing. Melody had wanted to know what it was like.

She remembered the cool marble. The impenetrable seam between those fine, chiseled lips.

This was like that and not like that at all.

Because Griffin was alive. Hard, yes, but not like marble.

He was so much better than stone.

So she entertained herself. She kissed him, angling her head this way, then that. But it was not until she slipped her tongue against that same seam, just to taste him better, that she shuddered.

"You have no idea how to kiss, do you?" His voice was raw. A scrape against the night, and deep into her, too.

"Teach me," she whispered.

Griffin made another one of those low, shockingly male noises that made everything inside her burn hotter. While between her legs, she felt slippery.

His hands moved from her shoulders and she protested that with a little noise, but only until he took her face between his palms.

Then Prince Griffin, Idylla's favorite scourge, set his mouth to hers.

And devoured her.

It was like falling. It was like tumbling through space, caught up in the waves of the sea and tossed this way and that, but it didn't ever end.

What he did to her mouth bore no resemblance to the kisses she'd given him, sweeping them away in a blaze of fire.

Griffin used his tongue, his teeth. He ate at her mouth, sometimes making more of those lush, dirty sounds that made her ache. That made this strange fever burn hotter, leaving her weaker and desperate for more.

Melody's life was built around sensation. What she could touch, what she could feel.

Nothing had ever prepared her for this.

For a mouth on hers, the scrape of his tongue, and the glory of the flames that licked all over her.

She was made new. She was forever changed.

She met the thrust of his wicked tongue, pressing herself against him with sheer, heady abandon, because every touch made it better. Hotter.

So much wilder and all-consuming than she'd ever imagined.

And she thought she might be perfectly happy to die like this—

But he stopped.

Griffin tore his mouth from hers, and then rested his forehead there, pressed against hers. It was a new spark. A different, quieter fire.

"I don't want to stop," she managed to pant out, surprised to hear she sounded as out of breath as if she'd just survived one of Fen's more brutal training sessions.

She could feel the change in his body, in the way he held her. He set her away from him, as if he was deliberately creating space. And then maintaining it.

"That should never have happened," he said, stiffly.

But Melody could hear what lay beneath it. All that same heat that was still storming through her, still making her burn with that wildfire that was only his. Why would anyone step away from that?

"Why ever not?" she asked, genuinely confused. "Aren't we supposed to be married?"

Griffin was turning her when she didn't wish to be turned. But there was no fighting it unless she intended to truly fight, so she allowed it. He tucked her hand back in his elbow and then, suddenly, he was walking her across the courtyard at a brisk pace he'd never used before.

As if he couldn't wait to be rid of her.

Melody didn't like the way that notion twisted around inside her.

"Am I to take the silence as an indication that we are not, in fact, married?" she asked tartly.

And as she did, wondered when exactly it

was she'd last pretended to be the wife the King and her own sister had asked her to be. When had she last cowered or cringed?

But she couldn't bring herself to do it. Not now.

Not when she could taste him.

Griffin did not speak again until he'd marched her to the door of her room.

"That should not have happened," he said again. Stiffly. Formally. Annoyingly. "It will not happen again. You have my word."

"I don't want your word."

"Nonetheless, it is yours. I keep my promises, Melody." She could hear the storm in him then, dark and ferocious. It made her heart clench tight in her chest. "Whatever else might be true about me, I keep my promises."

"As good men do," she whispered, though she shouldn't have.

Griffin made a low noise, but he did not reply. Instead, he turned swiftly and left her there, half fire and half fury, to burn out on her own.

CHAPTER EIGHT

THE WIFE HE'D never wanted and shouldn't have noticed much now he had her...was driving him mad.

It was the morning of New Year's Eve. As was his time-honored tradition, Griffin was chasing out the old year with the kind of punishing workout he usually reserved for whipping himself into shape after disappearing into too much debauchery for too long. Who could have predicted that a spate of abstinence would make the particular punishment he doled out to himself on this day...worse?

He ran faster, as if—with enough intensity and speed—he could outrun it.

Her.

It was one of the island's rare stormy days, keeping him cooped up inside when he would have much preferred to run up and down the hill from the palace to the beach. He liked the palace's private access road that ensured he could test himself as he pleased without causing a public commotion. He liked to tell himself bracing stories about his desire to pit himself against the elements, and that wasn't entirely untrue.

But a deeper truth was that his house had never felt so small, when he knew full well it could happily sleep eighteen.

Because Melody was everywhere. Even here, in the gym he doubted she'd set foot in, he was sure that he could catch her scent in the air. Or hear a hint of her laughter.

She was a ghost, haunting him wherever he went. And the worst part of that was that she was not dead like the others who called his name on dark nights. She was fully alive, flesh and blood, and living under the same roof.

"I was given to understand that this would be a sophisticated arrangement," he'd said coldly one night.

His nightly ritual of sitting in his study, brooding out the windows, and *not* drinking himself into oblivion because he was past that now he was married, had been interrupted. Again.

By the unsolicited appearance of his wife.

Griffin had not been pleased to discover that she did not need to be guided around the house, carefully ushered from room to room—and, more importantly, more easily left in said rooms. It turned out she could find her way on her own, which meant she...did.

"I think it would be difficult to get more sophisticated than the Idyllian Royal Palace," Melody had replied airily, standing there in the doorway as if she intended to become a fixture. "Isn't that, more or less, the definition of royalty? Sophistication by default and decree?"

"I was referring to our marriage." And the sound of his own, tight voice hadn't helped Griffin any. His bride was an onslaught all her own. "You have an entire wing of the house. Why aren't you in it?"

"You know why not."

She'd smiled at him, sweet and guileless the way she always did, though he knew better, now.

Melody might look like an angel, but she wasn't one.

Or more precisely, she had no desire to remain one.

"I have already told you that there will be no repeat of that unfortunate night in the courtyard," he'd told her with all the suppressed outrage he had in him. Because that had been a close call. Too close. He should never have allowed himself to succumb to temptation. He was furious with himself. And she didn't help matters. "There is no requirement that I produce an heir, Melody. Therefore there's absolutely no need for this marriage to be consummated."

"But—"

"You have already tried every possible method to convince me otherwise," he'd gritted out.

He'd stood up from his chair because it was entirely likely that she would try one of her other tricks, as she liked to do. The night she'd come and settled herself in his lap. The night she'd come wearing what she'd tried to claim was merely her usual nightgown, sheer and see-through and—but he refused to go there.

His bride might not fear his appetites, but he did. "If you will not protect your own virtue, I must."

"I'm more concerned about yours," she'd replied, there in the doorway with one hand against the doorjamb and the light playing over her lithe, lean figure—

Stop. Now.

"No need," he'd growled at her. "I possess none whatsoever."

"I only mean that this sudden valiant attempt at abstinence might actually do you harm." She'd tilted her head in that way he knew, now—though he still couldn't quite believe it—meant mischief. "Aren't you afraid that it will all go…blue?"

"I doubt very much you know what *blue* is," he'd all but barked at her.

Only to see, in return, a wicked smile take over her lush mouth. "I feel confident, however, that in this case I know what it does."

On his treadmill now, staring out at the sullen rain that pounded against the windows before him and stole his usual view of the ocean, Griffin picked up his speed.

But it didn't help. Nothing did. He might not have *gone blue*, as Melody had so inelegantly put it, but he wasn't right. He wasn't secure at last in his own goodness and virtuousness, which was the entire point of this exercise.

He could *taste* her, still. He woke in the night with the sheets twisted around him and his sex hard and heavy. While images that ought to have shamed him shined too bright and too real in his head.

God help him, it had barely been a week.

After he finished punishing his body, he tried a cold shower. But it turned out even frigid temperatures didn't help. His whole body turned blue beneath the icy spray—except one, specific part.

As usual.

While he dressed, then had his breakfast and spoke with his staff about the usual concerns he intended to ignore, Griffin accepted the fact that there was a part of him that liked the fact this wasn't easy. That the wife he hadn't chosen was more to him, already, than a piece of furniture or an inherited heirloom he was expected to care for, like all the rest littered about this house. That she had turned out to be far more of a temptation than he'd anticipated when he'd acquiesced to the marriage Orion had been threatening since his coronation.

He'd expended a lot of effort convincing the world that he'd allowed that particular part to lead him around for years. When, in truth, he'd simply indulged himself without limits, because he could. Now fiction had become fact and indulgence was out of the question.

Griffin supposed that was poetic. And no one had ever claimed poetry was meant to be *comfortable.*

If being a good man was easy, he told himself—sternly—as he headed toward the palace proper, there would be more of them in the world.

"Your marriage was meant to settle you," Orion said, sounding entirely too amused, when Griffin presented himself in his office. "I must tell you that you do not look particularly settled."

"On the contrary, brother." Griffin stalked to his preferred chair before the fire and draped himself across it like the libertine he'd been for years. And ignored how little he wished to lounge about bonelessly these days when everything inside him was so… fraught. "I have never been more at ease."

Orion's lips twitched. "Clearly."

"And what of your marriage?" Griffin asked. Demanded, really—taking advantage of the relationship only he had with Idylla's moral, upstanding, remote new King. "You've only been married one week. Most newlyweds would be off on a honeymoon somewhere, reveling in their new commitments in the time-honored fashion. Instead, you must host the traditional banquet and ball tonight and, as ever, ransom yourself to the demands of your duty."

"Is that an inquiry into my well-being?" His brother eyed him, seeing far too much, Griffin was afraid. "Or a complaint about your own situation? I didn't realize you and Melody enjoyed the sort of relationship that would require what a honeymoon normally delivers."

And the dark look Orion threw his way, as if Griffin's reputation swirled around him like a thick winter cloak…rankled.

Despite himself, Griffin could hear Melody's voice from that night in the courtyard that he was trying so desperately to forget.

Why must there be catching up or competing? she'd asked.

Why indeed.

And suddenly, on this final day of a strange year, it seemed important to him to find out— once and for all—if Orion was aware that Griffin *chose* to be dark to his light. That it wasn't who he was, it was who he had become. Deliberately.

Certainly, he had been exuberant in his youth. He had also had a decorated military career, something that would have been impossible had he spent even half as much time whoring about as it was reputed he had. And he had gone out of his way to downplay his military experience in all the interviews he gave, because that wasn't what the kingdom wanted from the second royal son. They had Orion for sober responsibility and the hope of a brighter future.

They wanted the spare to be *fun*.

"Do you imagine that I'm incapable of controlling myself if I wish it?" he asked.

Not nearly as lightly as he should have done.

His brother laughed. "I have no doubt that you *could* control yourself, Griffin. I do wonder whether or not you *will*."

"You asked me to marry a sheltered innocent who knows little of the world and even less of men, unless you count her loathsome father, which I do not," Griffin growled. "No, Orion, I do not require an extended honeymoon to slake my lust all over her fragile body. But thank you for thinking the best of me."

Orion lifted his head and fixed that particular stare on him that usually encouraged his underlings to...rethink.

But he had already committed himself to this ill-considered course, so Griffin stayed as he was, lounged out in a chair before his brother's fire. The very picture of careless indolence and self-indulgence.

He was good at that.

"I don't believe I accused you of anything," Orion said after a moment. The offended monarch in his gaze, if not in his voice. Not quite. "Is that a guilty conscience talking?"

Griffin had been about to apologize. But

now…he thought again. "I'm astonished you think I have a conscience. Surely not. After all, the whole of Europe knows I am little more than a cardboard cutout replacement of our late, unlamented father."

Orion only eyed him. And then, after a moment far more tense than it should have been, sighed. "I know you'll keep your promise to me, Griffin. As you have kept every promise you ever made to me. It is the Queen who is less certain."

"Perhaps if she had spent less time writing tabloid stories about my exploits across the years she would have less to worry about now."

He expected his brother to bristle at that, but Orion only smiled. He stood from his desk, and came over to the fire. Then he took the seat opposite as if settling in for a cozy chat, and all of this was so unlike his usually grim, workaholic brother that Griffin found himself…thrown.

A sensation he ought to have been used to, after all the time he'd spent with his bride lately.

Because unless he was mistaken, his brother, the uptight King, looked…relaxed.

"I told her something similar myself," Orion was saying, still smiling. "But you've met Calista, of course. She can't be *told* something."

But Griffin noticed that his brother sounded affectionate when he said that. As if that was not a flaw in his Queen, but a virtue.

He couldn't take that on board. Not from Orion, who had made a great many sweeping statements about the obedience he would expect from the woman he'd been required to marry, thanks to a deal their father had made. Threats of imprisonment on remote islands and so on, should Calista fail to fall in line. Griffin hardly knew what to do with evidence of *affection*.

He returned instead to the matter at hand. "Does Calista truly believe I will harm her sister?"

"Of course not," Orion said, so easily and so swiftly—so matter-of-factly—that something inside Griffin twisted in on itself.

He understood that if his brother had answered in any other way, or taken time to think it over, it would have irreparably damaged something in him. And that understanding landed in him with the full force of a blow.

It took him a moment to realize Orion was studying him. "It is the habit of a lifetime, nothing more, to concern herself with her sister's affairs. Calista has always seen herself as Melody's champion. And how do you find her? Your wife, I mean. Not mine." His smile took on a different sheen. "How is she adapting?"

"She's been blind since birth, Orion," Griffin said gruffly. "There was no *adaption*, only her life. She has never had to find something that was lost."

And he bit back what he'd been about to say—which was that Melody was perfect to him as she was. Maddening, yes. Shockingly uninterested in his notable good works on her behalf and not at all what he'd expected. But there was not one thing *wrong* with her.

Not a single, solitary deficiency.

He tasted copper and made himself smile instead. "I think she's doing beautifully."

"I am pleased to hear it. Calista will also be pleased."

"I live to serve."

As this was, in fact, true, Griffin could see no reason why it all seemed liked a collar around his neck just then. He told himself it was the constraints of duty, that was all. He would happily kill for his brother. But that was a different thing entirely than day in, day out, dutiful appearances.

Or marriages.

"I will see you later tonight," he said stiffly to Orion, unwinding himself from his chair and standing as if he meant to leave.

The stranger who now inhabited his brother's body, relaxed and at his ease, only lifted a brow. "You cannot be serious. Why on earth would you attend the New Year's ball?"

Griffin stopped on his way to the door, surprised. "Do I not always attend the New Year's ball?"

"Because you could have nothing better to do than dance attendance on your family when you were single. You are no longer single." His smile shifted and his gaze sharpened. "Perhaps you and your new wife can continue to…not have your honeymoon."

And Griffin did not precisely bare his teeth at his brother, his liege and King. But he wouldn't call it a smile, either.

He took his time heading back across the wet, cold courtyard to his house, where his staff was no doubt fluttering about, forever in the process of attempting to corral him into attending some or other dull function he wished to avoid.

The thought of it, in fact, made him move a little quicker, because he couldn't think of anything he would like better just then. A bit of corralling. Duties he was forced against his will to perform—it all sounded like bliss because it wasn't mooning about over his wife like a lovesick calf.

God help him, he'd become the very thing he hated. Soft and sentimental.

Too much like his mother.

When Griffin knew better than to allow such weakness in him. The former Queen had been no match for horrid King Max. He had been neither faithful to her nor particularly solicitous where she was concerned, and she had wilted in such conditions. Griffin's earliest memories were of her tears.

And then of the sad, lonely way she'd escaped her fate—taking her own life.

Whatever Griffin had become, he had chosen it. He had embraced it. Unlike his mother, so incapable of rising to the challenge of her tumultuous marriage, Griffin had met his role and made it his own. He was not and never had been a victim of circumstance.

Until now.

He had been so sure he knew what he was getting into. He had met Calista's sister once before, and she'd seemed so small and slight to him. She had cowered in her chair, half-feral with her hair like a curtain, and he'd thought—very distinctly—that she needed someone to take care of her.

Not himself, mind.

But when his brother had suggested—in that way of his that was not, in fact, a suggestion—that Griffin make good on his promise, and quickly, and with Melody, he had warmed to the idea.

He could prove, at last, that he could care for something so tender, so delicate. That he was better than the role he'd played all these years. That he was as in control of leaving his disreputable past behind as he'd been in creating his reputation in the first place.

What he hadn't counted on was Melody.

The rain had soaked him through on his walk back across the courtyard. He took his time changing, then made his way to his offices. But when he arrived, it was to discover that his staff had dispersed into the wet afternoon.

"You always dismiss the staff on New Year's Eve," his personal aide said, sounding baffled. And looking at him as if he'd come in with a selection of extra heads.

"Things have changed," Griffin said, attempting to sound dignified.

Or he had, which was far more disconcerting.

His aide gazed back at him. "Would you

like me to call them all back, Your Royal Highness?"

This time, there was no doubt about it. Griffin was not smiling. He was grimacing and trying to put a spin on it. "Of course not. You might as well take off yourself."

And then, for the first time in as long as he could remember, Griffin found himself... at loose ends.

It was humbling, really, to consider what a huge amount of time and energy it had taken to conduct his life and affairs as he had before. Or so he was forced to assume, since the lack of his usually overstuffed and heaving social life seem to echo in him like an abyss this afternoon.

Then again, perhaps he was brooding again. Because all the parties he'd used to attend were still occurring, in their usual forms. He had made stern announcements that he was to be left alone after his marriage, that was all, and he was a royal prince. His announcements held some weight for those who wished to curry his favor,

That didn't mean *he* couldn't dip into his old life as he pleased. If he pleased.

But even as he thought that, Griffin realized it wasn't what he wanted. The parties. The people. The endless jostling for his attention that, if it suited him, he pretended to believe was genuine feeling. He stood in his ancient house, the rain beating against the windows and gray straight through, and tried to imagine immersing himself in that world again. The world he'd considered his before Christmas.

Now it seemed like someone else's memory, fading quickly into insignificance no matter how he tried to draw it back.

Not only because he'd made a promise to his brother to avoid scandal.

It was her. It was Melody.

She'd kissed him, out there in the dark. She'd put her hand over his mouth. She made him ache, she disturbed his sleep, and he did not understand how this woman who could quite literally not see him…saw him best of all.

Griffin was a man with so many acquaintances, so many so-called friends. He had famously never met a stranger.

But he had always felt like one.

Until the least likely person in all the world…recognized him, somehow.

He didn't understand it.

But Griffin accepted the fact that left with nothing ahead of him tonight but empty hours, the ceaseless rain, and the dawning of a new year whether the world was ready or not, the only thing he was at all interested in doing was finding his wife. And that somehow, this thing that should have been anathema to him—his arranged marriage to a woman he should have had no interest in at all—in no way felt like a downgrade from his usual activities.

He decided he might as well embrace it.

He wouldn't touch her, Griffin assured himself as he found himself prowling through the halls of this sprawling, empty house. He didn't need to be led about by his desires after all these years of pretending he was a slave to them. He had no intention of allowing such a thing. But that didn't mean he couldn't... talk to her.

The simple truth was that he'd never met another person like Melody.

Because there was no other person like Melody.

As he walked, the rain beat against the windows as if it was washing off the year. And Griffin thought of how he'd wanted nothing more than to take apart his brother for suggesting that Melody was in some way impaired.

When Griffin knew better.

He had been sitting at pompous, tedious

dinner tables like the one the other night his whole life. Not once had anyone seen the faintest shred of anything in him he did not wish them to see. But she had.

She had seen *him*.

Then he'd tasted her. Barely.

But one taste of Melody, and Griffin was changed. Rocked. Reduced to cold showers and long runs, neither of which helped at all.

It was as if he'd never kissed a woman before.

He was not focusing on that, he told himself sternly as he found his way to her wing of the house. He would go to her, that was all. Ask her if she wished to join him for a drink. Tea, perhaps, if that was what she fancied on a gloomy evening like this one.

They would talk. She would once again prove herself far more mysterious than she ought to have been. And if, deep down, he acknowledged that the prospect of having tea with his almost completely untouched bride was far more appealing to him than any of the parties he knew were raging across the island right now—or would be, should he call and indicate an interest in attending one—

Well. That was no one's business but his.

He was headed toward her bedchamber when he paused. A strange noise reached his ears, rising now and again over the sound of the rain outside. A curious thump. Then another. A kind of…gasp.

Following the sound, he walked farther down the hall toward what had once been a conservatory for a long-ago princess who had preferred to secrete herself amongst her plants and herbs rather than spend her days ingratiating herself at court. Griffin had always felt a bond with his ancestress, though he had no affinity for plants and hadn't been inside the conservatory in years.

But there was no mistaking the fact that the noises he heard came from within.

An exhalation. A grunt. Something that sounded heavy, hitting the floor.

He eased open the door, wondering if his aide had been mistaken and there were still staff about the place, engaged in renovations of some kind. Not that he could recall authorizing any—but then, sometimes his staff took matters in their own hands rather than bother him with minutiae.

The door opened soundlessly, though it wouldn't have mattered if he'd slammed it open. And shouted while he was at it.

Because what was happening inside did not stop.

Griffin stood there, dumbfounded, as he attempted to make sense of what he saw. What was occurring right in front of him.

He couldn't.

It simply wouldn't penetrate.

Because it was impossible that his sweet, fragile, occasionally mischievous but clearly trembling and terrified wife, who also happened to be blind was...

Fighting.

There was no other word to describe it, inconceivable as it should have been.

Melody and that aide of hers were engaged in a lethal hand-to-hand battle, and Griffin might have hurled himself forth, thinking Melody under attack—

But she was landing her fair share of blows. She was attacking whenever she had an opening. With precision and clear intent.

It looked almost like an elegant dance. They threw each other, grappled on the floor, punched and kicked and never took their attention off of each other.

His bride, who clung to his arm as if an ocean breeze might carry her off, flipped in the air. She aimed her kick at the other woman's face, and when her opponent ducked, corrected in midair and then took them both down.

Punch, block, kick.

There was not one part of Melody that trembled.

And all the things Griffin had been blocking out seemed to flood in on him then. The way she'd seemed to challenge him, then cowered in the next moment. How lithe she was, how deceptively lean. How remarkably at ease with herself, as after her day of tea with society's worst, when any truly fragile creature would have crumbled. The muscles in her arms he'd felt and then dismissed, telling himself that was likely part of some or other therapeutic thing he'd assumed she must do.

This did not look therapeutic. It looked like art.

Melody not only didn't tremble, she was magnificent. Every kick, every strike, told him truths about who she was. Every easy, offhanded flip from the ground to her feet showed him that she had been hiding in plain sight from the start.

He could feel that beat in him like the drums of war.

But what he focused on most, just now, was that whatever else Melody was—chief among those things a liar—she was not fragile.

She was not breakable.

She was not any of the things she'd pretended to be. None of the indisputable things that had kept him in check.

Griffin felt the hold he'd had on himself crack into pieces, then disintegrate. There and then, like so much ash in the wind.

He didn't think he'd moved, or made a sound, but he must have. Because one moment, the two women were engaged in the most elegant brawl he'd ever seen. Then next, they froze, both of their heads whipping in his direction.

And he knew that his bride could not see him. His head knew that. But his body reacted as if those lovely sea-colored eyes were moving all over him the way he knew his own gaze moved over her.

"Prince Griffin," said her aide, not quite landing the appropriate bow.

But Griffin's eyes were on Melody.

Who, for the first time since he'd met her, looked utterly out of her depth. He could see the difference now, and maybe one day it would be funny, how deeply she'd deceived him. How she'd played the blind girl he'd expected to see, and he'd seen only that.

But he rather doubted he would ever find anything funny again.

"Griffin," Melody whispered. His name

almost a question. Her voice shaky, and this time, not because she was acting.

He could see that clearly.

And despite himself, despite how little humor he found in this—or because of it—he laughed.

It was a dark thing, wild and stirring, bursting out from the deepest part of him.

"My poor, deluded wife," he said, hardly aware of what he was doing, so focused was he on her. On how she stood in a fighting stance, not cowering or collapsing or trembling at all. The lies she'd told him battered at him, but now he knew the truth. He could feel that like her hands wrapped tight around his sex, as if the only thing he'd ever been was an animal. But this time, he did nothing to hold himself in check. "You should have known better. I might have been better than I pretended to be, but I was never all that good."

"I don't know what that means."

And something in him roared in triumph that she sounded off balance. That she wasn't quite so sure of him, after all. He wondered if she would try her act again. If she would cower or cringe, or do any of those other things he now saw, so clearly he couldn't believe he'd ever fallen for it—had been fake.

Lies in the flesh.

He'd seen what he'd wanted to see. But now he saw her.

There was no going back from that. God help them both.

"You will," he told her, menace and need warring inside him and turning into fire. "You'd better prepare yourself, Princess. Because I was happy to protect an innocent, but that's not you, is it?"

"Griffin…" she began, but his name in her mouth only made it worse.

He heard it as an invitation he intended to take.

"I have no reason at all to protect a liar," he told her, while the fire in him burned bright and tasted like victory. At last. "Least of all from myself."

CHAPTER NINE

MELODY COULD FEEL a beating thing, a wild exultation *this close* to panic and yet not quite, and couldn't tell if it was her heart or his.

"Leave us," Griffin ordered Fen, his footsteps ominous against the polished floor as he moved further into the room. Melody could feel him coming like a storm. "The Princess and I need to discuss a few things. In private."

"Perhaps it would be better if I stayed," Fen replied.

It made a deep sort of shiver rattle its way deep into Melody's bones. Because Fen was the least nurturing creature Melody knew, and given who she knew, that was saying something.

This could only mean it was worse than it seemed.

Her own heart beat so hard then, so loud, she thought it might leave a scar on the outside of her chest.

And still his footsteps came closer. Melody tried to imagine what Griffin must look like, bearing down on her. That beautiful face she'd felt beneath her hands taut and grim. Both of them unchained, finally, from this game they'd been playing all the while.

If the normally unflappable Fen was apprehensive, Melody should have been terrified.

But she knew that wasn't the thing that bloomed inside her, thick and ripe.

"I'll be fine," she murmured to Fen. "Truly."

She had no idea if that was true, so she did what she could to stand balanced on her bare feet. Ready for whatever might come at her— or ready to counterattack, anyway, which amounted to the same thing. She'd learned to punch and kick quickly, as all white belts did. It had taken her a great many more years to learn how to be still.

To wait.

"Godspeed, then," Fen muttered from beside her.

Melody didn't try to find her way back into the weak little character she'd been playing. She doubted it would work this time.

And on a deeper level, she didn't want to.

Because she wanted him to see *her* for once.

Had she sensed him? Had that been why

she'd felt so much fierce joy in this particular session? Why she'd jumped higher, punched better? Had she known all along he was here?

Melody knew he was here now, certainly. She could *feel* him as he stalked toward her, temper and heat. And she couldn't bring herself to shrink back down into palatable size.

She had no idea what to do with the storms she could feel snap and howl around them, but she knew she couldn't pretend any longer. It already felt like years since she'd agreed to play her role. Decades since she'd found the whole thing amusing.

Something in her whispered that she would pay for this, later—

But she heard Fen close the door.

And in the next second, Griffin was there. *Right there*, looming over her, wrapping the storm tight around them both.

Melody should have been afraid. But instead, she felt as if she was expanding. As if her ribs couldn't contain all the things she felt, and none of them was fear.

"It never fit, did it?" Griffin seethed at her. She could hear rain pounding down against the great domed ceiling, high above. But here, between them, there was nothing but thunder. "All this time, you were playing me. Letting me think I was protecting you when it seems, Princess, that you could take on the better part of the Royal Guard without breaking a sweat."

"Only if they got lippy with me," she replied.

The way she would reply to anyone. No breathiness. No cloying sweetness.

No act.

He laughed again, that wild, dangerous sound, as if he relished this as much as she did. No mask. None of that tinkling, polite, brittle laughter. No pretending she was meek when she was anything but.

"Did you have any intention of telling me the truth?" he demanded, his voice soft and close.

She didn't mistake the softness for weakness. Not when she could hear the fire in it. And could feel it crackling all over her skin.

"Because here is what I think you do not realize, my innocent bride." She expected him to grip her again, with those marvelously hard hands of his, but he didn't. Griffin prowled around her instead, walking in a tight circle. And she could feel, too distinctly, the touch of his gaze on every part of her. She felt a flush wash over her, head to toe and back again. "Or is that also a lie?"

"My innocence or our marriage?" she asked,

though it took her a moment to track what he was saying when she was far too caught up in the thunder. The fury.

His voice was a lash. "Pick one."

"I never had the luxury of being innocent," Melody told him. She concentrated on her stance. Feet on the ground, knees soft, hands loose at her sides. "Not in my father's house. He didn't get to be the King of Tabloid Filth by prizing purity. But there are different ways to lose innocence, aren't there?"

"I am primarily concerned with one."

Melody sighed. "No, despite training like this since I was very small, I am still in possession of a hymen and the virginity to match. A treasure beyond all others, or so I have been led to believe. Though I should say that this is mostly by default."

"Default?"

"I will confess to you, Your Royal Highness, that had I been given the opportunity or permitted the company of men, I would have handed off my precious treasure long ago. Sex always sounded far more interesting than random hoarding."

She heard what sounded almost like another laugh, as if he couldn't believe she'd said that. "Tell me—what did you hope to gain by pretending you were a fragile thing I might break if I looked at you directly?"

The exhilaration in her burned hotter. "I thought we covered this already. Beauty and the Beast, of course. Everybody loves a fairy tale. Particularly with sad little virgins, for some reason." She shrugged, too aware of his scrutiny. Her skin felt stretched tight and far too hot. "I'm afraid I don't make these rules."

"Did you really believe that I would fall for this?" That sounded rougher. Darker. "For the rest of our natural lives?"

Had she believed that? The truth was, Melody could hardly recall her life before this. Before him. Marrying him had changed everything. It had liberated her from her parents' house. It had opened up her world—even if, regrettably, it had mostly been opened to poisonous society types and tedious stately dinners. It had taught her that she, too, could yearn not only for concepts like freedom but for one very specific man. His flesh. His mouth. *Him.*

She hadn't known any of that when she'd walked down that aisle. How could she have?

And more, how could she have imagined this *need* inside her—that made her want nothing more than to tear aside the pretense and show him who she was, no matter what happened?

Calista has always told you that you were reckless, Melody reminded herself. *Apparently she was right.*

"It isn't about what I believed," Melody said. Carefully. She tracked him as he came back around to face her once more, seething and furious and deliciously male. "It's what you wanted to believe. I'm not the one who needs this fairy tale, Griffin. You do."

"Haven't you heard?" And he was even closer then. He was so *big*, the blaze of his temper so hot, that she could sense a kind of humming in what scant inches he'd left between them. She could feel that humming inside her, marking her, thrilling her, making her tremble. "There are fairy tales to go around in Idylla these days. The King has made it so. No one will pay the slightest bit of attention if this one turns out a little tarnished."

His hand came to her nape, tugging her head to his.

And then—at last—his mouth came down on hers.

Claiming her.

Possessing her.

Taking the storm that raged around them

and pouring it into her, then making it worse. Or better. Or both at once, leaving her spinning even as she clutched at his shirt to keep herself upright.

Because his kiss was an onslaught. A form of attack. Melody knew that.

But she thought she might die if he stopped.

He kissed her and he kissed her, and the way he plundered her mouth bore no resemblance to those kisses in the courtyard.

She shook, and this time out of a different kind of fear. She wasn't afraid of him. But he was...unleashed. And despite all her talk, she had no idea if she could handle all the raw power and sensuality that poured out of him, and into her.

No matter how much she wanted exactly that.

Melody was wearing loose workout pants and a close-fitting T-shirt, because she and Fen had agreed that there was no point raising suspicions by bringing any actual, formal gear. And it had been so interesting to train like that, in light, stretchy fabrics that allowed her a different understanding of the things her body could do.

And now, that same performance fabric offered no barrier whatsoever to the man who lifted her up, held her high against his chest, and then pulled her legs around his waist to settle her there. Wrapped around him like the vines that circled the columns in her parents' atrium.

Never once lifting his mouth from hers.

For long, desperate, drugging moments, it was like a battle. Melody fought him, though she hardly knew why. Only that she liked the familiarity of a fight. And she wanted to get closer. Deeper. Wilder.

She wanted things she couldn't name.

Griffin bore her across the room, toward the furniture that she and Fen had pushed back into the embrace of the plants, the way they always did when they trained in here. Then he took her down with him, so her back was pressed into one of the low couches.

But he came down with her.

Her legs were still wrapped around him. Her mouth was still fused to his. And as he settled, hard and huge between her legs, that relentlessly masculine part of him pressed tight against the place she ached the most, something in her...

Changed.

Surrendered, something in her whispered, though she wouldn't know. She never had before.

But she shifted, so quickly it made her

dizzy, from the kind of fight she'd always known and loved and considered a part of who she was to...a melting thing.

A sweet, wildfire burst of molten release all through her body.

"Hold on, Princess," Griffin growled, his mouth moving from hers to find its way down her neck, finding her pulse and toying with it until she shuddered. "You might know how to fight. But this is my game, and I know how to win."

And then he took her over.

There was no other way to put it. No other way to feel. She was melting and melting, and he conquered her.

Thank God.

His hands moved with skill and certainty. He pulled the shirt she wore up and over her head, pausing to shrug his off, too. Then he pressed his naked chest against hers, and that...was a delight. A mad, careening bloom of sensation.

Her nipples hardened at the contact, and then he used his palms there, as if he was trying to see the expression that she would make.

And her breasts responded, the proud ridges standing tall.

He laughed at that, a wicked sound.

Then he used his mouth.

And Melody…lost track of herself.

There was only sensation. There was only fire and need. He stripped her, pulling off her loose pants, and making a deep noise in his throat when she was naked before him. He took a moment while she shook, lying there before him, and it was only when he returned to her that she realized he'd taken his own remaining clothes off, too.

And then…it was a symphony. His body was so different from hers. His hair-roughened chest, so heavy and solid. The lean, hot weight of him, bigger and broader and all of it somehow delightful and perfect and alien and *right*.

He took his mouth and his hands to every part of her. Every last millimeter of her flesh, until she was thrashing, her head back and her fingers gripping whatever part of him she could reach.

Melody was already moaning when he got to that slick place between her legs. He traced her wetness with his fingers. Then he tasted her with his mouth.

Then he claimed her, completely, burying his head between her legs, eating her whole until Melody exploded.

She hadn't understood.

And she was sobbing, so she couldn't tell

him. She writhed and she bucked, and all Griffin did was hold her down and lick into her, until she exploded once more.

She hadn't *understood*. It had been like colors, the things she'd read about flower petals blooming and little deaths and a great many waves washing over and over and over a person who was likely shaking while it happened. She'd comprehended the *idea*. She'd known the *concept*.

But what Griffin did to her was not a *notion*. It was flesh. Blood. It was her bones like jelly and her body no longer hers, no control and no desire for any. It was *yes* and *more*, salt and tears, and a joy so intense it took her breath.

And then, as he found his way up the length of her body again, he used his fingers. It was a revelation made of flame and steel. No longer testing her wetness, but this time, finding his way inside her. Melody felt the stretch. The faint burn.

But she couldn't analyze it. She couldn't catalog the particular sensations the way she always did, then file them away with the rest.

Melody didn't want to learn the shape of him. She wanted to lose herself in him, or she already had, and there was nothing to do but allow it.

To glory in it.

To surrender herself completely and worry about it later.

He began to thrust in and out of her with his fingers, and that was so amazing, so astonishing, that Melody didn't know what to do with herself. She was making noises she didn't recognize. She flushed, hot and red, like a fever—but this one felt almost too good to bear.

But her hips seemed to know things she didn't, rising to meet those hard, seeking fingers. His mouth was at her neck. She felt the graze of his teeth on her collarbone.

And everything was this. The rise, the fall. The thrust of his fingers deep into her body. Steel and fire, flesh and blood. His mouth a hot demand. Her own sounds a betrayal and a song at once to this rough, wondrous music.

Then, finally, Griffin took her mouth again, kissing her deeply. Until his tongue mimicked the thrust and retreat of his fingers, and that was too much.

It was all *too much*—

And this latest explosion made her stiffen, everywhere, until she thought she might shatter.

Then she did shatter.

And when she was herself again, Griffin

was gathering her beneath him. He pulled her knees up and wide.

Melody could feel something wider and blunter than his fingers press against her softness. And she knew.

She had wanted this. She had dreamed of sex, that funny word that seemed so strange and sharp when all of this was…hot and physical, wide and deep. It was everything and too much and not enough. It was flesh and fantasy, surrender and hope. It was—

Griffin twisted his hips and thrust his way deep inside her.

And this time as she bucked against him, it wasn't another one of those explosions. It was a different shattering—and the shock of pain.

She blew out a breath, then another, and his hands were at the sides of her face, brushing her hair back.

"Breathe," he ordered her. "The pain will ebb."

She obeyed him. She believed him.

Melody tried to pull in a breath, then let it out again, but he was on top of her. He must have been holding himself up on his elbows, but that didn't take away from the press of him. That huge male body of his was sprawled out on top of her, holding her where she was. Keeping her there.

More than that, anchoring her in that place where they were connected.

Griffin seemed content to hold himself there forever. Something about that made her...not anxious. Nothing like anxious. But still, she wriggled her hips, experimentally.

Sensation walloped her, raw and huge, and she froze again. And panted a little.

But almost in the next moment, she tried again.

It was the same, only this time she was sure that there was something in the punch of it that she liked. Or wanted to like.

Melody knew pain, after all. She remembered the first time she'd been hit in the face—the shock of it, the emotional response. And then, years later and a great many more strikes and blows to the face—because that was how a person trained—it wasn't as if getting hit changed any.

What changed was that she knew how to take it.

And here, now, she figured she should apply the same principle. Lean into the sensation and find out what it was.

So she did. And the more she moved her hips, the more the intensity changed. It didn't lessen, but it didn't stay put. It seemed to move through her until she felt it, everywhere. And there between her legs, she couldn't decide if she was sore or scared or gluttonous.

The more she moved, the better it felt.

"Better?" Griffin asked, his voice a rough, spicy growl that merged with the sensations inside her and made them...*more*.

"Better," she managed to say. "Good."

He made another low noise. Then he gathered her in his arms again, dropped his face to her neck, and began to move.

First slow. Easy.

But every time she adapted, raising her hips to meet his thrusts, he changed the rhythm. Faster. Harder. Deeper.

It was too much. It was not enough.

She wrapped her legs around his waist again, not sure if she wanted more or if she wanted to hold herself together somehow, and he grunted his approval. And somehow that let her surrender all over again, losing herself in the building storm.

He found her breasts with his mouth, and still that pounding. That rattling, slick, intense thrust and retreat.

And the more she gave, the better it got.

Until eventually, everything began to tighten again. Everything focused on the place where they were joined, and it got wilder, and hotter, and too intense—

And she was suddenly afraid that whatever was coming for her, she couldn't take. She couldn't fight it. She couldn't *survive* it.

"Melody," Griffin said at her ear, his voice dark and wicked and beautiful. "Let it happen."

And it was as if she was waiting for that. For him to make her feel safe again, even in this.

She felt the punch of it first, a wallop that should have made her cry. Or perhaps she was crying already, but she didn't care, because her body was arching up into it. The rattle and the roll, the madness and glory rocked through her then.

Making her fall apart even as she was, for the first time in this searing heat, whole.

And still he pumped himself into her, thrust after thrust, until he roared out her name.

Then together they shook, and together they fell, and then, for a long while, there was nothing but breath.

And even that seemed near to impossible. Too much to bear.

The world crept back in. It felt aggressive.

Everything was different now. And yet, as far as Melody could tell, great swaths of the population ran around doing this all the time. So much and so often that they grew bored of it, or opted out, or any number of other things she hadn't really understood when she'd read about them and certainly couldn't imagine *now*.

It was physically painful to remind herself that if even a tiny fraction of the stories told about Prince Griffin were true, *he* went about doing exactly this the way some people brushed their hair or had a bath.

The world no longer felt aggressive. It was crushing.

"Well," Melody said brightly, though he was still sprawled over her. She couldn't tell which one of their hearts was pounding so hard it hurt, but she had a good idea. "Thank you. I was beginning to think I would die without ever understanding what sex was."

Griffin shifted and once more she felt his hand on her face, brushing back her hair. She was tempted to imagine that was tenderness. She felt herself melt all over again.

But when he spoke, his voice was all condemnation. "You have no idea what sex is. That was a palate cleanser. Did I not tell you to hold on?"

"Yes, but—"

There was that laughter again, dangerous and wild. It swept over her, making her skin prickle. "We're just getting started."

And he was still so deep inside her, it was like they were one.

She didn't mean to make the sound she did, something like surrender.

"I'm going to take you apart, Melody," Griffin said softly, a kind of dark promise. And she could feel him grow even harder, again, deep in the clutch of her body. As if every part of her, inside and out, was his. "Lie by lie. Until I'm done."

CHAPTER TEN

"HAD I KNOWN what the process of exposing lies entailed," Melody said some weeks later, "whether of omission or otherwise, I would have made it clear from the start that I was keeping things from you. The very first night, in fact."

She was exultantly naked, stretched out in Prince Griffin's bed, the wildfire within her sated. For the moment. A state she'd found herself in almost constantly as the first weeks of the new year wore on.

It was already the best year of her life.

Melody reached out with her hand across the rumpled sheets, searching for that glorious indentation that was Griffin's spine. She had come to a deep appreciation of a man's back. *His* back, to be more precise. She had clung to that back, dug her nails into it, drummed her heels against it. She had kissed her way across one side, then the other.

Thinking about the things she'd done made her want to do them all over again.

Griffin sat on the edge of his bed as he often did, and though she could feel that same dark, brooding force field of his all around them, she found it difficult to hold onto much of anything but joy. Until these weeks, she'd had no idea that joy could be a physical thing. It could surge in her veins, flood her whole body. It could sing in her chest and set fire to her limbs.

Oh, yes. This was a marvelous year, indeed.

She found him, and felt that humming electricity arc between them, the way it always did. Melody blew out a soft little breath at the buzz of it. Then she traced a lazy pattern over those powerful, hard muscles, down to the place where his hard, honed body met the surface of his wide mattress. A body so different from her own. She thought she could spend a lifetime reveling in their differences and never tire of it.

It was convenient that a lifetime was what they'd both signed up for, then.

Tonight had been like any other night in her new life as a royal princess. They had gone out to yet another engagement, the way they did most nights of the week. One thing that had changed, though Melody was not entirely certain what it meant, was that when home they no longer had their meals together. Griffin no longer doted on her, gallant and courteous, or walked her places at his snail's pace.

Which was not to say he was rude. But if she was to look for him, then find him in the house of an evening, Griffin no longer wasted time talking.

At first that had suited her. Having discovered the astonishing truth about sex, and how endlessly magnificent it was, all she wanted to do was drown herself in it.

Her new husband had been only too happy to oblige, despite his initial talk of lies and taking her apart. She chalked that up to the intensity of it all. All these weeks of it and she still didn't *quite* believe that she could really live through it, until she did.

It was like suddenly learning, after all this time, that she had access to a brand-new sense. All that sensuality, all that heat and greed and fire, worked together to make her feel like the four she already used were... different with him. Better when they were naked and he was inside her.

She almost felt she had never known her body until now.

As January wore on, however, Melody had

begun to notice things other than screaming his name and exploding into sensation—though slowly, she could admit. The fact he no longer seemed interested in conversation, for example, when before it had been as if her every word had fascinated him.

Tonight she'd spent the long evening out at another formal dinner, paying attention to the interesting undercurrents swirling all around them. But when she'd tried to describe them to Griffin on their drive back to the palace, he had instead pulled her over his lap, got his hands beneath her skirts, and had her sobbing out his name instead.

Once inside their home, he had carried her upstairs to his rooms. He had stripped her naked and had taken her once more, hard and fast against the wall of his overlarge shower while the water beat at them, enveloping them in a slick embrace of steam.

She hardly remembered how they had gotten back to his bed, where she knew she'd slept for a time, only to wake when he pulled her close once more, surging into her before she was fully awake the way they'd discovered she liked a little too much.

A person could cry out so much and so long that it no longer left her voice husky in the mornings, it turned out. Melody couldn't think of another way she might have learned that. And now she couldn't really imagine her life if she *hadn't* discovered that.

It was still the middle of the night. Griffin's royal bedchamber, where Melody spent most of her time these days, had walls of windowed doors on three sides and no curtains. The morning sun poured in, warming and waking her each day, usually to discover him gone and the bed cold.

There was no warmth on her face now. And he was still there.

And when he did not respond to her hand on him, it occurred to Melody that perhaps it was finally time to pay attention to more than the things they could do to each other's bodies.

Or you could press yourself against him and kiss his neck, and see how quickly you find yourself beneath him, she argued.

But it was one thing to find herself so sensually overwhelmed that her skin felt too sensitive. It was something else to deliberately avoid a topic because she'd grown accustomed to sensitive skin, and wanted only more of it.

"Is something the matter?" she made herself ask.

"Go back to sleep, Melody," Griffin ordered her, his voice low.

She sat up instead, dropping her hand from his back, which felt like a grievous loss. "If that was meant to be soothing, it failed."

"Heaven forfend that I fail you in some way. Can the foundations of our marriage based on lies survive? Unless, of course, I make you come again."

Something inside Melody twisted at that, a sharp and unpleasant flash too close to actual pain. He sounded darker than usual. Forbidding, even.

She began to count back. And as she turned over these past weeks in her head, she realized with some shock that he had changed completely on New Year's Eve. Night and day, in fact, while she'd trailed around after him, desperate for more.

It was like when she'd learned to read Braille. It had opened up a whole new world, and she'd wanted to do absolutely nothing else but explore.

Possibly that made her something less than the ideal wife. She sat straighter and decided she would make up for that now. Since Griffin had obviously done all these things before, it stood to reason he hadn't been quite so drunk with the joy of it.

Though she would have sworn he had been.

"What if, for a change, we had a conversation?" she suggested.

And a cold sort of flush washed over her when she heard his short, bitter laugh.

"What is there to discuss?" Griffin's voice was even darker and more forbidding than before. "You lied to me. That's the beginning and the end of everything."

Melody wished she had paid a little more attention over the years to her sister and the relationships Calista had spent so much time building, buttressing, or fixing. But she hadn't. She'd had no expectation that she would ever have those things, and besides, she'd always found Calista's friendships, contacts, and endless talk of networking...silly, at best. It was nothing but games and misdirection.

Melody preferred the simple eloquence of a fist. A kick.

But now there was a heaviness in the room, his words felt like a bruise, and she had no idea what she was doing.

"I have already told you why." Or she had tried. She had not told him that his brother had personally asked her to pretend she was fragile, as even she with her inadequate grasp of relationships had concluded that would not help anyone. "I had no idea what kind of man you were. Or how you would treat me. Of course I kept a few tricks up my sleeve."

"I would not call what you did 'a few tricks,' Melody. What you did—everything you did—was a carefully calibrated misrepresentation of who you are. There's not one fragile bone in your body."

He had turned while he spoke and now he crawled over her. Melody fell back, though she could have fought to stay upright, because her body wanted nothing more than to surrender to him. To whatever he threw at her. Again and again and again.

She could feel the cage of his arms, and then the weight of him, pressing her down into the mattress. And surely there was nothing wrong with this. With them. Maybe this was how relationships were built—using whatever common language was available, and this was theirs.

Melody had long since become fluent.

Between them, she could feel the heavy weight of his arousal that she was beginning to think filled him with despair even as it made her shiver with delight.

"Aren't you pleased?" she whispered then, her lips near his. "Isn't it more fun to make each other shake instead of worrying that I might shatter without warning?"

"I detest liars," he said, a growl against her mouth. "There is not a single member of my family who did not lie to me. And now you, too. The woman I will be tied to for the rest of my days."

She shifted her hips, smiling at his sharp intake of breath.

"And you, of course, are a beacon of honesty at all times," she murmured. "Even when, for example, you pretended for years to be dissolute and shallow when you are neither of those things. Not entirely."

"You have no idea what you're talking about."

"Griffin—" she began, and this time without the complication of her hips, or her soft heat against the steel of him.

But he didn't allow it.

He kissed her fiercely, wildly. And despite herself and her notion that she ought to *do something more* the way a wife surely did, Melody thrilled to it.

The way she always did.

Griffin flipped her over, muttering dark demands into her ear as the huge, hard heat of him slid home. Melody groaned.

And he took her that way, a ferocious claiming, without another word.

The next time she woke up, the morning light was pouring in. It danced over her skin, spreading its warmth wherever it touched, but Griffin was nowhere to be found.

Melody wanted to go and find him, to demand that he explain to her what was happening. What she'd missed. Her heart was pounding too hard, as if she was exercising when all she was doing was lying in a bed, alone.

But she made herself breathe. She made herself think.

And reminded herself that strategy won far more fights than brute force ever did.

So instead of forcing the issue, she would train. And wait.

That night, her staff dressed her in yet another one of the ensembles that, in all likelihood, the Idyllian press would fawn over tomorrow. It was another thing Melody had come to accept as these weeks rolled along.

Because while Melody had lost herself completely in carnal delights, Idylla had also fallen in love. With their King and Queen, who everyone agreed were a bright new light, sweeping out King Max's darkness. And more, with Prince Griffin, whose sudden Christmas switch from bad boy to besotted husband set the island to fluttering and swooning.

Still.

Melody herself was considered fragile, certainly. But the public loved her. For every aristocratic woman who delivered backhanded compliments, Melody was seen as being that much closer to full-on sainthood. *An angel of redemption*, the papers cried.

Her staff had taken to dressing her accordingly.

"What am I wearing?" she asked Fen on her way out.

"A halo," her friend replied, laughter in her voice. "As always."

"I am your redemption, apparently," Melody told Griffin later, in yet another car on the way to yet another engagement.

A moment she had chosen precisely because he could not silence her the way he normally did. Not if he wanted to parade her into the dinner looking like an angel. Smudged lips and wild hair would not give quite the same impression.

She could tell from the tension in the car that he knew it.

Griffin was sprawled out across his side of the plush back seat, taking up far too much of the available space and brooding so loudly Melody was surprised the driver couldn't hear it through the glass.

"It's a nice story," he said. Eventually and with ill grace. "But I think we both know the truth."

Melody found she was growing weary of this. There were so many more enjoyable things they could be discussing. Like what he did to keep his body in such delicious shape. Or what else he could teach her. She found it an endless delight that she'd married a man who had quite literally done it all, and could show her.

"What does it matter if I am less breakable than you imagined?" She had to remind herself to keep her impatience out of her voice. Somehow she knew he would not appreciate it. That, in turn, might possibly lead to less sex, and she couldn't have that. *Focus*, she ordered herself. "You were famous for how much sex you had. Quality and quantity, apparently. Surely you cannot have imagined that you would spend the rest of your life as a monk?"

"I wanted to," he bit out, shocking Melody so deeply that her half-formed decision to interrogate him...disappeared.

"But why? Why would anyone want that?"

"Not all of us are granted the opportunity to pretend that we are holy, clean, and pure." Something dark and painful was between them then, and laced through his voice. The car felt hot with it. "I don't expect you to understand."

"But I do." She reached out a hand, meaning to touch him. His face, or his chest—but he grabbed her hand in midair, stopping her. Melody curled her fingers over his, then, and held on. "Do you know what it's like to be held up as a symbol for others when all you really want is the luxury to be a person like anyone else?"

"Do *I*? You forget who I am. Do *you*, Melody?"

"I have always been my father's excuse," Melody shot back at him, still holding his hand in the space between them, gripping his fingers tightly. "His embarrassment or his curse, depending on the year. Meanwhile, my sister watched me train for years and knew full well that I have always been capable of defending myself. More, she knew I enjoyed doing it. Yet somehow, my life became her burden to bear. A problem she was required to solve, whether I felt I required a solution or not."

"You cannot possibly compare our experiences." His words were like bullets. "My life has been a public spectacle outside my control since my mother showed me to the world from the palace balcony two days after my birth."

"You think I don't know what it's like to forever live according to others' expectations?" Melody laughed. "I don't consider myself disfigured, disabled, or any of the other words people use to describe things they don't understand. I am me. And still, I was asked to hide that. To play up what everyone else thinks is a liability. To make sure that everyone around me, especially you, would treat me as an object of pity instead of a woman. What else do you think a saint *is*?"

His hand tightened against hers. She could feel his pulse, hard and hot.

"These past weeks, I thought that finally I'd been given the opportunity to be everything I am to a person who isn't Fen," Melody continued, her voice a little more intense than it should have been. A little too intense to pretend she wasn't emotionally involved in this, like it or not. "I like to play games, I'll admit. But I thought we stopped. Yet we didn't, did we? You called me a liar, and ever since, you've cut what we could be in half. If you can't protect me, you deflect with sex.

If you no longer think I might fall apart, you take me apart, but only in one way. There's a name for this, you know."

"You can call it what it is. Consequences," he gritted out. "The consequences of your actions and nothing more."

"Or, possibly, something like a madonna/whore complex. Just throwing that out there."

"I don't have a complex," Griffin growled. "What I have is a fake marriage."

He dropped her hand.

Melody wanted to reach out again, but she didn't. And it hurt.

Try some strategy, she snapped at herself. *Unless you* want *him to keep treating you like this*.

"But you have always had a fake marriage and you have always known that it would be exactly that," she said. Reasonably, in her opinion. "You married a perfect stranger by order of the King himself, on scant notice and with no opportunity for argument. How did you think that would play out?"

"I married a half-feral waif who had been locked away in a basement and needed rescuing. I made her a princess." Griffin's voice was darker than she'd ever heard it, and still it hummed in her, bright the way she thought light should be. "Only to discover she was neither of those things, never was, and never will be."

"Then what am I?" she asked as the car slowed. She could feel Griffin gathering himself, putting his public mask back into place, and she wanted to rip off whatever halo she was meant to be wearing and toss it. At him. "Because I would have thought that a secret ninja princess would be the perfect companion for the kingdom's favorite Prince, who covers what good he does with all that charm and too many playboy antics. A secret saint all his own."

"Secrets are nothing more and nothing less than a sickness waiting to claim its casualties," came Griffin's reply, as if it was torn from him. "And there is no time for ninjas tonight, Melody, secret or otherwise. The ambassador wants nothing more than to tell happy stories of hope and redemption, just as my brother does. Our only obligation is to embody those stories in public, lies or no lies."

"You do know that it is possible to do both," Melody said. The car stopped. She heard the driver open his door. And told herself the drumming of her pulse was something other than a strange panic at these things he was saying. "Surely you and I decide what our marriage is in private, no matter what show we must put on for the world. I don't believe you need redemption, Griffin. And if you do, why must it only come with abstinence? Why can you only be a good man if you're denying yourself—"

"Because there are consequences for actions," he threw at her, and he sounded so… stark. "There is always a price to be paid, Melody. Maybe your life has been sheltered in such a way that you have never had to learn this lesson. But you will now. You should never have lied to me. But you did. We are what *you* made us."

"I'm not the one who put me on a pedestal in the first place," Melody said softly. "You did. You wanted me to be a saint so you could be, too. Now you blame me for falling when I am who I ever was."

"A lie," he growled. He leaned closer, and she thought she felt his lips at her temple, a brush of heat that made her think of loss and fire, need and grief. "What you are, Melody, is a lie."

She knew she had his attention now, electric and intense. Melody could feel the full impact of it on her, like hands pressed tight to her skin, seeing things she would have preferred to keep hidden.

"Maybe I am." She shook her head. "But Griffin… If you don't have someone to blame, who are you?"

CHAPTER ELEVEN

HER QUESTION HAUNTED HIM.

Griffin felt he should have been used to that by now. Everything involving Melody was a haunting of one form or another. First he'd wanted nothing but to put his hands on her. Wanting had kept him awake, made his days an exquisite torture, and taught him precisely what kind of man he was. Now he wished only that he could lose himself in the madness and heat they generated between them. He told himself it was better that way. That it was all there was and ever had been.

He should have been happy.

Griffin was an unlikely monk, and well he knew it. It was a role that could never have fit well, and he'd found it almost unbearably suffocating in the course of a single week. *One single week*, he growled at himself, lest he was tempted to forget.

To make up for it, he'd spent these weeks

since discovering Melody's perfidy doing little more than teaching her one sin after the next.

But it turned out that wasn't enough, either.

He had taken her home from the ambassador's house that night, forestalling any further commentary or haunting questions on her part the same way he always did. Because he called her a liar, he knew full well she was one—but their bodies fit together like magic.

And despite himself, Griffin knew full well there was no greater honesty, no sweeter truth, than the spells they cast together. Over and over again.

Until he was having trouble remembering why it was he couldn't let himself trust what he felt. When they were naked, fused into one. Slick and hot and so perfect together it sometimes hurt.

"Your marriage has been even more successful than we dreamed," his brother told him one pretty day. "I must congratulate you on a job well done."

It was the end of January and the brothers stood out on the palace balcony, which had long been used for any number of official appearances from the royal family. His parents had stood right here and presented each of their sons, the heir and the spare in turn, to the nation with all attendant fanfare. Griffin liked to tell himself it was his earliest memory when, in truth, he suspected he'd seen the photographs and newsreel and had incorporated them as a personal recollection he could not possibly have had at two days old. But a grand presentation to an adoring crowd was as good an origin story as any for the kingdom's charming rogue of a prince, he'd always thought.

Though it seemed to scrape at him today.

"I'm delighted, as ever, that my personal life can serve the crown," Griffin replied to his brother.

And though he'd intended that to come out with a certain dark humor, he could tell he missed the mark. Orion's gaze slid to him, then returned to the crowd. They both stood at attention, waving, while below the crowds chanted and cheered. Griffin kept his usual public smile plastered to his face and, today, found it a chore.

"Is there trouble in your personal life?" Orion asked mildly. *The King* asked, Griffin corrected himself. "Anything I should know?"

"I suspect you already know," Griffin retorted. Again, more harshly than necessary. And certainly more harshly than was wise out here in public, where there were always telephoto lenses.

He remembered Melody's words in the car that night. *What do you think a saint is?* she'd demanded, throwing the question at him with the first real spark of temper he'd seen in her. Something he should have celebrated, because wasn't that what he'd claimed he wanted? Honesty no matter the cost?

Today it felt like a price too steep to pay. All of it.

Orion didn't reply, too busy waving while below, the Royal Guard performed a particular march to celebrate Idylla's Armed Forces. Griffin regretted saying anything. More than that, he regretted that he no longer seemed to have control over himself. He knew whose fault that was.

Who are you? Melody had asked him. *If you have no one else to blame?*

He couldn't seem to shift that question off of him. It sat on him like a weight, thick and heavy.

When the event was finished and it was time to retreat back into the palace, he found himself hoping that some crisis had cropped up and Orion's aides would sweep him off to tend to important matters of state.

No such luck.

"What is it you think I know?" Orion asked, dismissing the staff waiting for him with a flick of his finger.

Griffin took his time facing his brother. His King.

"You too?" he asked. Lightly, he told himself, though there was too much ice in it. He shook his head. "Is there no end to the lies you plan to tell me, brother?"

Orion stiffened. "I don't think I—"

"I understand your need to protect me when we were young," Griffin said stiffly, aware that he was crossing a long-held line. Knocking down a wall the two of them had left standing between them for a reason. "The responsibilities of your position have always come with all kinds of knowledge I doubt you wanted yourself. I don't blame you for not sharing things out of a need to shoulder the greater share of the burden. It is why you are already a great king. But this? Asking my wife to lie to her own husband? How can you possibly imagine that falls within your purview?"

To his astonishment, his brother looked stricken.

"At first I thought it was a lie perpetrated on you as well," Griffin forged on, not waiting to hear what Orion might offer as a defense. "That it was Calista who advised her sister to hide the truth about herself. I would put nothing past the Skyros family, after all. But I quickly realized that Calista was not her father or you would not have married her. Because I trust *you* enough to know your own wife."

He realized as he said it that he had not spoken so harshly to his brother since long before Orion took the throne. But he did nothing to walk it back.

"I don't think you understand," Orion began, in that careful voice that won over fractious members of his court and made his ministers sigh with pleasure.

Griffin was not appeased. "You are mistaken. I understand completely." He raised a brow, his gaze steady. "You don't trust me to keep my promises, though I have never broken them. You know how I feel about lies, and yet you did this anyway. I have always thought that I was lucky because whatever service I provide my King is part of the joy I have in my brother. Thank you, Orion, for proving that joy is a one-way street. It is better to know that than not."

Orion stood as if facing a firing squad. "That is not what I was doing. I didn't think of it as a lie. It was a bit of misdirection, that's all. Nothing more and nothing less than the harmless white lies anyone tells at the beginning of a relationship."

"It was not up to you to decide," Griffin bit.

"I am your brother first," Orion said, his voice rough. And nothing like careful. "Always."

"Alas, Your Majesty, I don't believe you," Griffin shot back.

And then, deliberately, performed a deep sort of bow more appropriate for lowly servants in the presence of the monarch than the King's blood. To his mind, underscoring the truth of their relationship. It was royal. It was municipal. But Griffin was a servant to the crown more than he was a brother to a king, and he needed to remember that.

Then he turned, quitting the room before he began to say even more things he shouldn't. He could feel them all bubbling up inside him, making a mockery of the character he'd spent a lifetime building, then playing. He was meant to be relaxed, at ease. He was the foil to his brother's upright morality.

But who was he when there was no one to blame?

He tried to shove that question out of his head, but his walk back through the palace made it impossible. Griffin had grown up here. He'd spent his life in these very halls. And yet all he could see today was Melody.

Melody clinging to his arm when he now knew she could probably run down these halls without incident. Melody tipping her face toward his. Melody with her hand over his mouth, telling him to smile, to frown.

Melody everywhere, like a tune stuck in his head. Giving him no quarter and no peace.

He let himself into the side door of his house and then stopped, listening for her. Listening to see if he could tell where she was and what she was doing that easily, because he persisted in imagining that if he knew what she was doing he wouldn't feel this *need* to go and see it for himself.

Yet once again, loath as he was to admit it, he felt drawn to her. As if he no longer had control over himself.

As if he couldn't stop himself from shoving his fingers deep into his own wounds.

Griffin took the stairs two at a time, choosing not to question his haste. His abominable *need*.

And he found her in her reception rooms, tending to the daily work of the social calls he suspected she found as tedious as he always had. He nodded curtly at the guards outside her door, then stepped inside without making a sound.

His wife—his secret ninja princess, as she called herself, and he should not find that so charming—was sitting on her usual settee, bathed in all that golden light. Griffin told himself that her inescapable beauty, her sheer perfection, shouldn't make such a racket inside him. He told himself he wanted it to go away.

It is only sadness, he told himself.

Because he knew the truth. Because it was lies. Because *she* was.

But when he looked at her, all he saw was her radiance.

As bright and as beautiful as any truth.

And it did not seem to matter how many sins Griffin taught her or how many times he practiced them upon her. It did not seem to matter how many times she broke apart in his hands, or screamed out his name, or rode him to a wild finish as if she was the one teaching him each and every one of the carnal delights he'd thought he'd mastered.

None of it touched her.

Melody was holding a cup and saucer before her in a crisp, elegant manner that made the two women sitting across from her seem almost embarrassingly gauche in comparison. And all she was doing was sitting there. Listening.

"I beg your pardon," she said softly when the woman who had been speaking paused to take a bite of one of her tea biscuits. "But I believe my husband has need of me."

When Griffin would have said she could not possibly know he was there.

And then it was all exclamations and fluttering as the two women—who he was certain he knew, though he found he could not focus long enough to identify them—scurried from the room in clouds of overexcited tittering.

"You do not normally show your face at these calls," Melody said when they were gone. Griffin indicated with a nod of his head that the remaining staff should leave, too. "Lady Marisol and her sister will dine out on your appearance for weeks."

"I don't know why I'm here," he ground out when they were alone.

Against his will.

Melody rose, then, nimbly moving around the furniture and making for him, unerringly.

Griffin still wasn't used to it. There was still something inside him that expected her to trip. To fall. Or to at least *look* as if she wasn't quite so sure of herself.

To need you, something in him suggested.

"There's nothing I can do about the fact I deceived you, Griffin," Melody said softly when she came to a stop before him. "I would apologize, but I'm afraid I'm not as sorry as you might wish me to be. In my position, I suspect you would have done the same thing."

Griffin didn't want to hear that. And he didn't want to think about it too closely, either, because he was afraid she was right. Arranged marriages weren't particularly out of the ordinary in his world. It was a widely accepted practice not only in Idylla, but in many royal and aristocratic circles around the globe. But it was different to walk into one as a woman.

Of course it was. Especially if that woman was blind.

"It had nothing to do with you," Melody continued as if she'd read his mind. "For all I knew, I was jumping from one fire to another. I don't regret protecting myself. I would do it again."

"Thank you for your honesty," he managed to say. And then, because he couldn't help himself, "Even if it is a bit late in the game."

And something in him seemed to shatter, even as he stood there. It was her scent, crisp and sweet at once. It was the smile he'd failed to keep on his face before the crowds. It was her, all of it, and now he knew her too well. The warmth of her skin. That smooth, glorious curve of her hip that could cause war and peace alike, and often did. The crushed velvet of her nipples and the strength in her thighs, particularly when she gripped him tight.

He knew too much.

And still Melody stood before him, something almost like a smile shaping her lips, her eyes so wide and the endless blue of the sea.

Griffin wanted things he shouldn't. Things he couldn't understand.

It never got better, that wanting. It only grew more intense. She was *doing this to him*, and still, she looked like an angel.

"It doesn't have to be like this," she said softly. "Does it? Can't we make it what we want it to be?"

"You don't understand."

Griffin expected her to sigh at that, the way she often did. Argue, maybe.

He could have handled that much better.

What she did instead was to reach over and slide her hand over his heart, as if she could hear the way it beat, jagged and painful.

"I want to understand, Griffin," she said softly. "But I can't unless you tell me."

"It was my mother," he said, when he was

certain he had no intention of speaking. It was as if the words were torn from him, and once spoken, he couldn't seem to stop.

He put his hand over hers, there against his chest, intending to peel hers away.

But he didn't.

Before him, Melody simply waited. Still and yet engaged. No longer pretending to cower or shake, and that seemed to punch in him. He would never have told this story to a fragile creature. It would never have occurred to him.

Melody was anything but.

"She used to tell me I was her favorite," he heard himself say, his voice as rusty as the words seemed when he'd kept them inside so long. "My brother had belonged to the crown since birth, but I was her friend. Her *buddy*."

God, how he'd always hated that word.

"As the years went by, she became more pale. Brittle, almost, the longer she stayed married to my father. She told me only I made her smile. Only I tethered her here."

Melody made a soft sound of distress. "That seems like an unfair burden to place on a child."

"Whether it was or was not, it was the only thing that kept her with us." Griffin ran his free hand over his face. "Everybody knows that my mother took her own life. But they act as if that was out of the ordinary for her. As if it was a one-time mistake gone too far." He shook his head, his throat suddenly thick. "It wasn't."

Melody only murmured his name. And he suddenly felt that her palm, lying there and holding his heart in place, was the only reason he was still standing upright. Telling this story he'd never told. The story he'd vowed he would never tell.

"She tried again and again," Griffin said, unable to stop himself. "And sooner or later, if someone wishes to go, they will. No matter how carefully guarded. No matter how loved."

"It's not your fault, Griffin," Melody whispered.

He looked at her, fiercely glad she couldn't see the emotion he feared was far too obvious, all over his face. Even as he was convinced that somehow, she knew anyway.

"I'm afraid you're wrong about that," he said, his voice steady with the conviction of all these years. The scar of it. What it had meant to him. What it made him. "My brother found her. But I left her. She promised me she would not do it, and fool that I was, I believed her. *And I left her.*"

Somehow, it seemed as if Melody's palm against his chest grew harder. Hotter. And there was something about the expression she wore that made a low sort of shudder move in him. *Protective*, something in him whispered.

But he thrust that aside.

"The only other person I have actively tried to care for in my life is you," Griffin told her, because what did it matter now? Why not lay all of this out, this grief and betrayal, so that at last what was between them would be clear?

Unmistakable.

And then, maybe, he could go about the business of putting himself back together when he still didn't quite understand how he came to be so broken in the first place.

"You're focused on the fact that I am not as weak as you expected me to be," Melody said, a faint crease appearing between her brows, making her look fierce. "But you made me feel safe. Me, Griffin. When I have never felt such a thing, anywhere. Or with anyone."

He wanted to hold on to that. He wanted it to mean something. When would he stop with all this fruitless *wanting*?

She blew out a breath. "No one fights the way I do, consistently and with years of intense practice, because they already feel safe.

I thought the only way I could ever feel like that was if I was actively attacking someone. If I was winning a real fight. But all you had to do was treat me as if I was fragile. As if I might be precious. And there it was."

This was excruciating.

"It was a lie," he gritted out.

"But don't you see?" She shook her head, that hand on him seeming to pin him to the wall when he wasn't touching it. "What would it really mean if you had saved a weak and fragile creature, more breakable than glass? Anyone could save such a girl. I could save twenty with my hands tied behind my back. Surely the victory is greater when the need is less."

He reached out to touch her, but only to grip her shoulders so he could set her away from him. Because he *wanted*, God how he *wanted*, and he knew better than that.

Telling Melody the story of his mother reminded him, forcefully, of the one inescapable truth he never should have let himself forget.

He had left his own mother to die.

What he had left was a promise to his brother and a wife he was sworn to protect, no matter what. He deserved nothing more.

And that meant, no matter who he blamed

or how he felt about it, that first and foremost he needed to protect Melody from himself.

Especially if she was foolish enough to feel safe in his presence.

"I never should have touched you," he told her, almost formally. "I betrayed both you and myself when I allowed the truth of who you are to cloud my judgment."

"That did not feel like a cloud to me, Griffin. It felt like clarity."

He ignored that. This was about keeping his promise to himself—the one he'd made the morning his mother had been found. That never again would he let anyone too close to him. Not when it was so clear that he couldn't be trusted.

"We will return to our initial arrangement. Wiser, I hope."

"We can't return to me cowering and cringing and you imagining that's real," Melody replied, matter-of-factly. And it kicked about inside him, the way she said such things. With total conviction and absolutely no fear. "So what is there to return to?"

"Something more civil than this," he blurted out. "The way marriages between people like us have always been."

Melody considered him for a moment that seemed to stretch out. And ache.

"If you make yourself a priest, riddled with the glory of your abstinence, would that make up for it, do you think?"

He stiffened as if she'd shot him. Some part of him would have preferred it if she had. He thought of the knife he'd carried in his boot since his soldier days, and how easy it would be to simply take it out, hand it to her, and let her do her worst. How much quicker and more elegant.

At least then there would be no waiting. No quiet tyranny of day after day of *wanting* all these things he couldn't have.

No more of this, he ordered himself. It was time to retreat into duty. Into the ascetic life he'd planned to live once he married. No scandals, no secrets, and none of this ruinous *passion*. That was a risk other men might take, but not him.

He should have known better. He had.

Now it was time to enforce it.

"You wanted to understand and I have told you," he said, scowling at her even as he drew himself up. She might think there was clarity in the way they'd come together, that howling, greedy madness, but he knew better. Clarity was clean. It was a kept promise, not a messy vow. "And it doesn't matter if you agree with my reasoning or not, Melody. This is how it will be."

He heard the ring of finality in his own voice and, for the first time since he'd seen a wild and cringing creature in his soon-to-be sister-in-law's company, thought he might actually be himself again. It was a gift.

He told himself it was a gift he wanted.

"Because you are the Prince?" Melody asked, a strange note in her voice. "You think you can order me around?"

"That and because I'm bigger than you. Either way, this ends here."

Griffin picked her up and set her back another few feet, so there could be no argument. And no possible impediment to him walking out of this room and into a quieter, more reasonable future.

"I hope that in time you'll see the beauty of this arrangement and understand the need for—" he began as he made for the door.

But the world was upended.

Something hit him, hard.

Then he could do nothing but lie there, blinking, as it slowly dawned on him that he was...on the floor.

He was on the floor of the main reception room, in fact. And his angel of a wife was standing over him, her hands in a position even he could see was decidedly martial.

More critical, to his mind, was the foot at his neck.

Not *quite* applying pressure.

Melody's hair had fallen down around her, and he was reminded once again of the first glimpse he'd had of her. His Eponine, and why was it he had forgotten that Eponine was more feral than sweet?

It was only as his heart thundered in his chest and the breath came back to him that he understood what must have happened.

"Did you...*throw* me?" he demanded, feeling tautly stretched between temper and astonishment, there on his back on the floor at her feet. And a host of other things he dared not name.

"You might be bigger than me, Your Royal Highness," Melody said, cool and calm as if she tossed men of his size this way and that all day long. "But might is only right if it actually works. Otherwise it's little more than ballast and can only make a hard fall hurt more. As perhaps you've discovered."

His head was spinning, and he wanted to blame the fall he'd taken, but he suspected it was her. Just her. "Melody—"

This time, astonishment warred with sheer

outrage as she applied pressure, lowering her foot as if to cut off his airway.

And the look on her face told him she just might do it.

"Enough talking, Griffin," she said, like a queen commanding the peasants. "It's my turn."

CHAPTER TWELVE

"IF I WERE YOU," Griffin seethed at her, simmering there beneath her foot in all of his male glory, "I would think very carefully about your next move."

Melody could feel a different kind of electricity in him. A kind of shock, climbing up her leg and fanning out to take over the whole of her body. It had been something like instinct to reach for him, to throw him.

To show him that unlike everyone else in his life, *she* would not be so easily dismissed by the kingdom's favorite Prince.

They were his press, his adoring public, even his brother. She was his wife.

Maybe it was time to show him what that meant. What she wanted it to mean, anyway.

"What makes you think I haven't already thought through my next move?" she asked, taking pleasure in the mildness of her voice. In the fact she wasn't breathing heavily after that throw, while his chest was still rising and falling rapidly. "If I were *you,* I might issue fewer threats after finding myself on my back, clearly no match for a woman one third my size."

"Is this the romantic poetry that you hope will change my mind and lure me back to your bed?" Griffin asked acidly. "It leaves something to be desired."

"Not all of us had access to your educational opportunities," Melody said, and even laughed. A real laugh, for a change, because they were alone and she'd thrown him and what point was there in wearing masks at this point? "While you were comparing and contrasting sonnets in fine universities, I was learning the poetry of movement. And of stillness. Better still, how to make myself unseen—especially when standing in full view."

He vibrated beneath her, temper and steel, and it moved through her like a caress. "You are not the only person who had to learn such things. And if you do not remove your foot from my throat, I cannot be held accountable for my actions."

Melody did not remove her foot. If anything, she applied more pressure.

"I am not the one dead set on pretending we are so different that we must exist in a monastic marriage for the rest of our days," she threw at him, fiercely. "Do you really think I don't understand grief? Do you imagine I didn't spend my youth tearing myself apart, wondering why it was I had been born with an affliction I couldn't hide? How hard do you suppose it was to choose to love my sister when it would have been so much easier to hate her, simply for being all that I am not?"

His hard fingers laced around her ankle, but she still didn't move her foot. "I hope you're not suggesting I'm jealous of my brother. Nothing could be further from the truth."

Melody was so used to hiding. To pretending to be less than she was.

But Griffin had taught her that there was no level of intensity he couldn't meet. And that was the Griffin she believed—the man who was as wrecked as she was, but still reached for more. The man who held her so close she felt as if she was inside him, too. The real Prince, dark and stirring and, most of all, hers.

She was tired of hiding. Of fighting on mats, with Fen, and never for herself.

Never for what mattered the most.

That ended here.

"What I'm suggesting is that each and

every one of us is filled with the same dark mazes, Griffin," she said then, the intensity of her feelings making her voice shake. "It doesn't make us special. It doesn't make us different or unique. What makes a person is what they do with the darkness inside of them. Because you can dress it up in any pretty words you like. You can blame your mother. You can claim you blame yourself. But at the end of the day, you and I both know that the real reason you want to keep us in these boxes of yours is because you're afraid. Of *us*, Griffin."

"If you do not remove your foot," he bit out, sounding far more vicious than before, "I will stop treating you with the courtesy my wife deserves and instead treat you to the sorts of things I learned when I was a soldier. You do not want that."

"I welcome it," Melody shot right back. "You speak of honesty? Then fight me. *Me*, the person who's right here in this room with you. Don't hide behind old promises and ancient guilt when you know as well as I do that what is between us is extraordinary."

She felt his hands grip her ankle tighter, and not entirely gently.

It thrilled her.

"I do not wish to be indelicate," Griffin

hurled at her, and she could feel the great blaze of him, there beneath her foot. She could feel it race up her limbs, making her shiver. Making her wet. Making her that much more determined to get through to him. "But you are not in a position to judge, Melody. You lack context."

"You're going to have to do better than that," she chided him. "Do you really think that you can insult me? My father is inferior to you in every conceivable way, save one. When it comes to insults, Aristotle Skyros is truly peerless."

Below her, she could feel the tension in Griffin tighten. He had to be reaching his breaking point, she thought.

And in the next moment, he moved.

It was sheer joy.

He tried to simply shove her away, moving her foot as if he could move her body that easily. Succumbing to that belief in his own superior power that Fen had always taught her about. *Even if they see what you can do, they will not believe it*, the older woman had told her. *It will not make sense to them. They will assume that because they are bigger they will always be stronger. That is a weapon. Your weapon.*

Melody broke his hold and flipped backward, hampered only slightly by the dress she wore. Despite the dress throwing off her form, she landed nimbly and evenly, laughing as her feet hit the ground.

"Come now, Griffin," she scolded him. "You're going to have to do better than that."

"I'm not going to fight you," he said stiffly.

"Why ever not? Are you afraid that I will best you? You should be."

He made a noise like thunder. "What will happen, Melody, is that I will hurt you!"

She danced closer. And then she punched him, hard.

Right in the solar plexus.

And waited until he pulled a ragged breath back in.

"No," she said, steadily. Intently. "You won't."

"I won't fight you," Griffin gritted out. "No matter the provocation."

"No sex." Melody kept her hands up as if, at any moment, she might strike him again. "No sparring. What remains, then, in this imaginary marriage you intend for us to have?"

"I don't care," he growled at her. "Just so long as it does not—"

"Hurt?" she prompted him. "But I think it will, Griffin. I am certain of it."

And this time, when she danced close again, she ducked beneath his arms. And stayed there, flush against his chest, her palms flat against the steel of his pectoral muscles.

"Melody..."

Her name was a warning.

"Here is a greater hurt, then," she said softly. "I love you, Griffin."

And for a long moment, he was silent. Still. Beneath her hand, his heart pounded, but it was as if he was once again made of stone. Impossible marble beneath her palms.

Deep inside her, something started to crack. Because if she could not reach him, then what? Had she truly exchanged one prison for another after all? She hadn't wanted to believe it.

"No," Griffin said at last. She had begun to worry he would not speak at all. And he sounded tortured when he did, making that cracking inside her go deeper. Wider. "You cannot. That is a darkness no one can penetrate, I promise you."

"I'm not afraid of darkness," she whispered. "I live there."

"Melody." Another warning, though this one more broken. "You don't know what you're saying."

"Close your eyes." And then she checked that he'd obeyed her, lifting her hands and sliding them over his eyes. She pulled in a breath, holding them there. "Stop worrying about the darkness. Think about your heart. Listen to your breath. To the sea outside, far below. To me, Griffin."

"Melody…"

But this time her name was more like a song.

She shifted up on her toes, closer to him, glorying as ever in the way their bodies fit so perfectly together. Whether they were dancing, fighting, or exploring each other on his wide bed, it was always like this.

As if they had always been meant to find each other.

"Feel this," she whispered, and then she kissed him.

And Melody knew how to kiss him now. How to tease him, how to tempt him. How to make them both shudder.

How to turn want into need, heat into fire.

She kissed him again and again, and she wasn't surprised when Griffin shifted, kissing her back. Taking control.

His hands moved into her hair, sinking in to hold her where he wanted her.

"This is not darkness," she said, tearing

her mouth from his. "This is love, Griffin. I suspect it always has been."

He dropped his head closer to hers, but he did not open his eyes beneath her palms.

"I wanted to give you the Prince, not the dissipated lout," he told her, there against her mouth. "And maybe it was easier to pretend it was the lie that made the difference. But it's *me*, Melody. I don't know how to be whole. I am one or the other, never both, and you deserve more than that. You deserve a real life. You deserve love."

"I deserve the life I've chosen. With the only man I will ever love." He tried to pull away but she slid her hands down to grip his neck, and held on. "You don't scare me. Your dark, your light, they are all *Griffin* to me. You speak pretty words and you make the crowds laugh, but all I hear is your heart. I always have. I always will."

She felt that cracking thing inside her, or maybe he was the one who shook.

Or perhaps this was the earthquake they'd generated, a tsunami not far behind, and as long as they were together like this—still that perfect fit—she couldn't say she minded.

"I couldn't live with myself," Griffin managed to say, "if I lost you too."

And the cracking, the shaking, intensified, but she wasn't afraid of it any longer.

"There is a simple solution to that," Melody told him. "Live with me without any rules. Love me without any boundaries. Forever, Griffin, so neither one of us ever loses."

And for a long moment, she didn't know if she'd reached him. She could feel the fight in him. The battle. Earthquakes and tsunamis, tornadoes and storms.

But he didn't pull away.

"You have no idea how much I want to believe that I might be capable of such things," he said as if each word cost him. As if they hurt. "How much I wish that somehow, I could even pretend to give you what you deserve."

"You have already made the scandalous Skyros sister a royal princess," Melody said, smiling against his mouth. "It seems to me there is no magic you can't perform."

She felt the fight in him...shift. Like the tide going out. His arms moved, but only to hold her.

"What am I to do with you?" he asked quietly.

And Melody's smile was so wide then, it threatened to split open her face. "I've already told you. No monasteries. No lies. We will do what we must outside these doors, but in here, when it's just you and me, why can't we be only and always who we are?"

"Why not indeed?"

Then Griffin was kissing her again, over and over. And when he shifted, lifting her into his arms, she thought he would carry her to one of the couches—but he didn't.

He shouldered his way through the doors, and carried her through the halls of their home, taking her to his bedroom.

"I've been playing a role my whole life," he told her as he set her down beside his massive bed. "I don't want to play it with you any longer. But I warn you, once I start this thing with you, I fear I will never stop."

"What do you think forever means?" she asked him, that smile still on her face as if it would never leave.

Griffin knelt down, his hands spanning her hips in a possessive grip that made her feel something like giddy.

"Princess Melody," he said, his voice deep and formal and the most beautiful thing she had ever heard, "I thought taking you as my wife was an act of charity, and it was. But it was not me who was bestowing that charity. It was you. I cannot compartmentalize myself with you. I cannot pretend. I want everything or nothing. And nothing will not do."

"I love you," she said. "And think, Griffin. We've only just started. We have our entire lives ahead of us."

"And with you, I want it all." He leaned forward and pressed a kiss to her belly, its own kind of promise. "With you, I will risk anything. Family. Happiness. Love."

Love. The word was like fire in her.

But the more she burned, the more it felt like pure joy, until she thought she might burst with it.

"Prince Griffin." And Melody's voice was thick, because these were vows. This was their real wedding, right here, where their true communion had begun. "With you, I can see. The life we will live. The family we will raise. The love that will grow stronger, day by day."

"Year by year," Griffin agreed, his voice rough with the same emotion that coursed through her veins.

"Because if it doesn't..." Melody promised him softly, sinking down on her knees before him and smiling all the wider. "Trust me, my beloved Prince. Feet on your throat will be the least of your concerns."

"I can't wait," Griffin said, and then he

gathered her in his arms, took her to their bed, and got started on their real marriage, there and then.

smoothed her in the sense, from here to then bed, and got married — or the real marriage, then and there.

CHAPTER THIRTEEN

OVER THE YEARS, Griffin learned many things about the woman he had imagined he was saving—only to discover that all along, he was the one who needed it more.

He had learned the safer she felt, and the more comfortable in his presence, the wilder and brighter the joy. Just as he had learned that she was in no way a morning person and should always be approached with caution and coffee.

Not in that order.

He moved her into his suite, not the least bit interested in the normal way things were done in marriages like theirs. The real truth was that there were no marriages like theirs. And while he and Melody could play any role the palace required, in this house, what they were first and foremost was in love.

Love, Griffin found, changed everything.

He found his way back to his brother, because he understood, now, the things that love could make a person do. He understood that Orion had thought he was helping, not hindering.

And he forgave not only his mother for leaving, but himself, too.

The joy got wilder and brighter all the time.

He and Orion, without consulting their brides, took it upon themselves to suggest—in no uncertain terms—that Aristotle Skyros remove himself from Idylla. For good.

"You cannot banish me," the horrible man seethed at his King.

"And he will not, as he is a good and benevolent king," Griffin replied, all idleness until he met the despised man's gaze. "But I do not think you would like it should the rest of the royal family feel compelled to take matters into their own hands."

Aristotle slunk off, never to be heard from again. It was impossible not to view his departure from the island—and his daughter's lives—as a triumph of epic proportions. Especially when his wife remained behind.

And Griffin watched as time did what nothing else could have. He would not call it a true healing, necessarily. But when Calista started giving Apollonia grandchildren, a mother found her way back to the daughters she had abandoned.

"I will never trust her," Calista said with a sniff after her first child was born, sitting in the private parlor where the four of them often gathered.

Melody shrugged. "I have always liked her more than you. She was kind enough."

"*Kind enough* is not kind." Calista smiled down at the newborn Crown Prince while beside her, Orion looked besotted. The Queen gazed at her sister. "Though I will admit, even she blooms without Father around."

"So would a desert," Melody replied.

And later, when they were alone, Griffin showed Melody precisely what he thought about *kind enough*. By being first deliciously cruel.

Then so kind she screamed.

"I think I'm ready for the next adventure," Melody said one night, when they had been married for five glorious years.

"You may have any adventure you like," Griffin told her with that gallantry that made her smile. And call him *Gaston*. "You already have."

They spent the bulk of their time dutifully representing the interests of the crown. They were mindful of their responsibilities. But they also took long, significant breaks, where they pleased no one at all but themselves.

Melody had wanted to explore the world, and he had taken her wherever she wished to go. They had jumped from planes, hiked up mountains, swum with dolphins. Griffin had lived more since he'd met Melody than the whole of his previous life.

The longer they stayed together, the deeper and better it got.

"I hope you mean that," Melody said then. They lay in their bed, the soft Aegean breezes playing over their naked skin.

She nestled against him. Then smiled.

With an innocence that struck fear into his heart.

Because whatever else his beautiful Princess was, a secret ninja or a wildly creative lover, she was never innocent.

"Tell me what you want and I will give it to you," he declared.

"You already have," Melody said quietly. "And in about seven months, you can meet him yourself."

Griffin thought that his heart could never beat that hard again. That he could never love more than he already did.

He kept thinking it, and he was always wrong.

As Melody proved twice more. Two perfect

princes and one remarkable princess filled this house of ghosts with laughter, bloodcurdling screams, and joy.

So much joy, it hurt.

You missed all this, Mother, Griffin thought years later.

All three children had been settled into their beds, some with tears and some with grace. And his wife appeared before him on her soundless, careful feet, her hair the way he loved it, wild all around her.

Fifteen years had passed since the day he'd carried her here from the reception rooms where the local ladies had long since learned not to poke at Princess Melody. Since the day they'd stopped being two and had become one, at last.

Since the day their true marriage had begun, and changed everything.

"I hope you locked them in," he said, grinning as she came to him. "Hellions."

"There is no point. It would work for one night only, and then Fen would teach them all how to break out. But I've thrown the bolt on *our* door, never fear."

"My beautiful, perfect wife." Griffin gathered her to him, holding her in his arms. "My Princess. What would I have done if I'd never found you? Who would I be?"

"Let's never find out," Melody said.

Then she wrapped herself around him, making that same, sweet fire burn bright between them, the way it always did.

And always would, hot enough to propel them straight on into forever.

Over and over again.

* * * * *

Enchanted by
His Scandalous Christmas Princess?
*You'll be sure to adore
the first story in*
the Royal Christmas Weddings duet:
Christmas in the King's Bed

*And why not lose yourself in these other
Caitlin Crews stories?*

Unwrapping the Innocent's Secret
Secrets of His Forbidden Cinderella
The Italian's Pregnant Cinderella
Claimed in the Italian's Castle

Available now!